Dirty Rich

BETRAYAL

NEW YORK TIMES BESTSELLING AUTHOR

LISA RENEE JONES

ISBN-13: 978-1723921117

To obtain permission to excerpt portions of the text, please contact the author at lisareneejones.com/contact.

All characters in this book are fiction and figments of the author's imagination.

www.lisareneejones.com

CHAPTER ONE

Mia

I pull my rental car to the gate of Grayson Bennett's beachside Hamptons mansion, and I stare at the keypad. The code won't be the same. It's been a year now. He would have changed the code and yet, instead of punching the call button, my hand trembles as I reach for the numbers. I key in the code I once used often and the gate begins to creep open. I grip the steering wheel, some part of me wanting to believe that Grayson left the code in place because he hoped I'd come back. Which is ridiculous. The man betrayed me. He never loved me. He hurt me, and yet here I am, about to stand on his doorstep and ask to come inside his home and domain.

I pull the basic sedan that I picked up in the city to avoid a chopper service, and pull it around the circle drive, stopping on the opposite side of the house, where I park under my favorite willow tree. The minute I kill the engine, my heart thunders wildly in my chest. I can't believe I'm doing this, but I am. I'm here. I'm doing this. I slide my purse over my head and across my chest to allow it to rest on my jean-clad hip. I'm not backing out now.

I climb out of the car and into a gust of chilly late-October wind coming off the ocean. My light brown hair lifts, and the chill on my neck has me snuggling deeper into my light blue sweater. I inhale the fresh scent of the ocean, the taste of salt on my lips follows and so do the memories of this place, of me here with Grayson. I can't believe how emotional this feels. Why can't I just get over this man? I *am* over him. This is just me reacting to a time in my life when this man stole my every breath. It's a part of me, just as he always will be.

With that mantra in my mind, I hurry forward and rush up the stairs of the understated mansion with three steeples and wood siding. My chest pinches with the realization that the last time I was here, Grayson had just inherited it from his late- father, a man I loved and respected. A good man with exceptional taste and standards. Raymond Bennett did nothing less than perfect, this stunning house included.

I stop at the door and reach for the bell, but my hand falls away, my lashes lowering, with the attack of memories that charge through my mind; the fight, the betrayal, the tears, so many gut-wrenching tears he didn't deserve, but there is also so much more—the history. The way he made me feel like I was his world when obviously I wasn't, but it doesn't seem to matter. I can't seem to forget him and standing here now, I can *still* smell his woodsy cologne and taste his passion and *my God*. My eyes pop open. What am I doing? I can't be here.

I should have just called.

I turn and head down the stairs, but my attempted escape comes too late. The roar of an expensive engine sounds moments before a black Porsche Boxster, Grayson's car of choice, circles the drive, and speeds toward me. I halt at the last step as he, in turn, halts the car directly in front of me. I hold my breath, preparing for the impact this man has always had on me, telling myself he won't anymore. I'm not the same person I was when we were together. I'm stronger. I'm harder. I'm more jaded.

I *won't* melt for Grayson Bennett.

He kills the engine and pops his door open, obviously not going into the garage. I'm here. He wants to know why. He unfolds himself and straightens all six feet three inches of his hard body, the wind catching in his thick, wavy dark hair, as my fingers often did in the past. He shuts his door, his unassuming, faded jeans and long-sleeved black T-shirt hugging every hard inch of a body that is just as perfect now at thirty-eight as it was at thirty-five when we met. Back when I was twenty-seven, his junior by eight years, and his wisdom and confidence inspired admiration and attraction in me.

He saunters toward me, his stride easy, but no less predatory, while oozing power and grace. He stops in front of me, towering over me despite the step down I have yet to take. He's close, so very close. My gaze sweeps the hint of gray in his neatly trimmed goatee that I like a little too much. My lashes lower, and I breathe out before I force myself to look at him, my stare colliding with his potent green eyes and even with all my inner dialogue about not reacting to him, I am. I feel every touch I've ever shared with this man right here, right now.

"Mia," he says softly, and I swear I feel his voice like a caress of his hand.

"Grayson," I say, and his name feels right and wrong on my tongue. So right. So *wrong*.

"I didn't expect you," he says. "*Ever.*" There is a sudden coldness to his tone that stabs me like a knife.

I'm an attorney and I'm good at my job. I maintain my control and I do it well, but I react now when I don't want to react. "This was a mistake," I say. "Forget I was here." I step around him and off the stairs, but he catches my arm

3

and turns me to face him. Heat radiates from his hand, up my arm, and over my chest and Lord help me, my nipples are hard.

"There are many mistakes between us," he says. "Don't make coming here and backing out another one."

He's right, but that's my only thought. I can't think when he's touching me. I've never been able to think when this man touches me. "Can you not touch me, please?" I whisper.

He releases me like I've burned him when he's the one who burned me, his jaw hardening, his eyes icing. "Let's go inside," he says, motioning me forward, and I know this man. I still know him so very well. I hurt him just now. Why do I care that I hurt him? He practically took a knife and cut me open.

And yet, I do. "Grayson," I begin, not sure what I'm about to say or if I'll regret it, but he cuts me off.

"Let's go inside, Mia," he orders, anger in the depth of his voice when he rarely allows anyone to see anger, but then, this is me and I was always the one that broke through all that steel and control. Or maybe I didn't. Maybe I just thought I did because nothing was what I thought it was with Grayson.

I head up the stairs and he doesn't pull the power play of following me. That's not his style. He's at my side, and we fall into step as we walk to the porch, giving me the façade of sharing control. You don't share control with Grayson. You just think you do. That's where I went wrong with this man. I thought I was different. I believed I shared control with him. I believed I shared a lot of things with him, but I didn't. He owned me and the problem is that I wanted to be owned, but those days are over. He will never own me again.

He opens his door, and I don't know why I do it, but I look over at him and when his eyes meet mine, I do just what I said I wouldn't do. I fall into the sweltering heat of our years of history and melt for this man in a way no other man has ever made me melt. I hate him. I love him. I hate him. And as if it somehow protects me from all that he is to me, I dart inside the foyer of his home.

CHAPTER TWO

$\mathcal{M}ia$

The past, two and a half years ago

I leave the first day of my job as an associate with my head spinning. The Bennett firm is a massive operation, expanding across the world, and even outside the legal profession, which I now know is driven by the heir-apparent son. Grayson Bennett apparently wants to rule the world and he's succeeding. It's exciting to have this much opportunity after being stuck in a small firm that had a ceiling, thanks to my finances forcing me to attend a small school part-time to get my law degree. Finally, I've opened doors to a better future. Finally, I have the chance to yank my father out of poverty in Brooklyn.

Exiting the elevator, I start thinking about the case that I was put on today and how to approach winning. I need to have a plan that helps the partner I'm working under. I need to prove I can handle my own cases, the way I did at my prior firm. I hurry toward the exit and push through the glass doors on a mission. Home. Work. Research. I turn right and collide with a hard wall with such force it rattles my teeth.

"Oh my God," I gasp, as strong hands come down on my shoulders, while my hands have now settled on the broad chest of a man wearing an expensive three-piece suit. "I'm sorry. I was—" I lose that thought as I look up into his green eyes and my lips part in stunned shock. He's gorgeous. Perfect. Overwhelmingly perfect.

"No apology needed," he says softly and oh so very intimately, or maybe I'm imagining that because *come on.* What girl doesn't want this man to speak to her and only her? "In fact," he adds. "I think this is the best part of my really crappy day."

I swallow hard. "I uh—don't know how to reply to that."

The man to his right clears his throat. "We'll meet you upstairs," he says and only then do I even realize that this gorgeous man is standing in between two other men, but I don't look at them. Not when *he's* still looking at me and ignoring them. Not when his hands are still on my shoulders. The two men leave.

"Have a drink with me later," my newfound sexy stranger says, a push that is almost a command in his voice. He's older than me, thirty-five I think, while I'm twenty-seven, and he radiates the kind of confidence I need to own myself. He's no associate. He's no subordinate to anyone and I like this about him.

"I don't even know your name," I say.

One corner of his really delicious mouth curves and he says, "You will tonight. If you show up. Meet me at Morrell Wine Bar at eight. You owe me the date for running into me, but I'll buy the wine." He reaches up and strokes my cheek. "You have beautiful blue eyes, by the way." And then he leaves me there, stunned and warm all over.

When I can finally walk again, I'm not sure what to do. He has to work for Bennett. Am I allowed to date a co-worker? I don't even know. I hurry toward the subway, and I try to reason with myself. He might not work for Bennett. Maybe he's just using their services. I haven't dated in a year. I've been too busy. I'm too busy now, but—there is just something about that man. He's inspiration for all I want and need to be. He owns who he is and what he is. You know this even without knowing him. I need to breathe that in, I need to have a glass of wine with that man.

⋙⟡⋘

Grayson

I'm packing up my office with one thing on my mind— the woman with the gorgeous blue eyes—when Eric walks in, his jacket gone, his sleeves rolled up to expose his tattooed arms. My father hates those tattoos, but then he doesn't understand that Eric isn't a master investor and project manager, because his father owns an empire that he walked away from. It's because of the depth of his life experiences; and those tattoos represent years in the military while his Harvard degree is a product of the mastermind with numbers and strategy he's proven himself to be over and over. More so, his honesty and character make him a friend I trust.

"Your father is on a rampage," he says. "He's pissed about—well—everything."

"That usually means people get things done right next time."

"True," he says. "Though I prefer your quiet intolerance." I round the desk and he offers me a folder. "Those numbers you wanted on the building acquisition in Atlanta. They look good. I'd do it."

9

"Then we'll do it. Make it happen."

"After you look at the numbers. We're good because we see different things on paper. I don't want to sign off until I know what you see."

I nod. "Fair enough. I'll let you know in the morning."

"You're going to see that woman."

"I am."

"She's a new associate."

I arch a brow. "You checked?"

"Of course I checked. You're a fucking heir to a billionaire who's just made his own personal billion."

"With your help," I concede, "we've both taken a chunk of change and turned it into a whole lot more for this place and ourselves. For me, that's living up to my father's expectations. For you, it's a 'fuck you' to your father."

"And I want many more," he says. "My job is to watch your ass. I emailed you her file and then some."

"I'm not going to look at that. I'll know all I need to know when I'm with her." I start walking. I'd suspected she might work for the company, which is exactly why I booked our meet-up in my apartment building, not the offices.

"For the record," Eric calls out behind me, "on paper she's one of two things: the best thing that ever happened to you or the worst."

I stop at the door and look at him. "Sounds like the beginning of anything new." I turn and exit the office, and I don't even think about looking at that email. There is something about this woman that speaks to me. I can't explain it, but I don't want it ruined. I want it pure and I want to learn about her from her.

My car service is waiting on me and in roughly ten minutes, I'm exiting in front of my Central Park building. I hand the doorman my briefcase and tip him well enough to have him ensure my bag makes it to my apartment safely.

Nix is a good man, who's been here the entire five years I have. I trust him. I always surround myself with people I trust, at every level.

I enter the bar, which is an intimate location with low hanging lights, a triangle-shaped bar, and booths lining the walls. I don't choose a booth. I head to the bar that allows me a view of the entire place and control. I also always choose control. I've barely sat down when the bartender sets my usual in front of me, an expensive whiskey they custom order for me. I'm not a man of extravagance by nature, but this whiskey is worth every dime I spend on it.

She walks in before I even take a sip, still wearing the same navy-blue suit dress that while conservative and appropriate for work, has a zipper that slides down the front. I noticed, but then I also noticed the tiny freckle on the corner of her eye. She looks around, scanning for me, and the curl of her fingers into her palms tells me she's nervous. She spots me and inhales a telling breath. Yes, she's nervous.

She walks in my direction and I watch every step, admiring her long, slender legs and the sway of her hips. I want this woman. I want her naked. I want her beneath me and I want to know who and what she is, and I have to know. I am a man with much to lose and she is too close to me and my company for me to wade blindly into anything. She stops at the seat next to me.

"Hi," she says.

"Hi," I say, finding her charming and sweet as few women strike me these days, and yet, intelligent. I see that in her eyes. "I'm glad you came."

She doesn't attempt to sit down. "I almost didn't."

"Why?"

"Because I have a lot on the line. I can't blow this job. I've been thinking about this and I need to know why you were at the Bennett building."

"Why does that matter?"

"Because I'm new there and I don't want to break any rules. So, before I sit down, I need to know if I really should."

I am a man who doesn't just like to trust people. I expect people to be honest. Because like my father, I'm honest, even when it makes my life harder. I like where she's going so far, but that doesn't mean my name won't show a side of her I won't like.

I stand up and my hands go to her waist. I turn her, placing her back to the bar, my body pinning her to it. "I appreciate your desire to follow the rules. Bennett allows inter-office relationships because I don't believe it's realistic to believe people can work together seventy hours a week, in a company this big, and never cross that line. I simply expect that they handle it professionally and let HR know."

She blinks. "I'm confused. *You* believe and expect?"

"What is your name?" I ask.

"Mia," she says, and like the good attorney she should be, she immediately circles back to her question. "I'm confused. You said—"

"I'm Grayson."

Her eyes go wide. "Grayson? As in—"

"Grayson Bennett," I supply.

"Oh my God." She pales. "Why didn't you tell me?"

"Would that have mattered?"

"*Would it have mattered?*" she asks incredulously. "Of course it would have mattered. I'm not trying to climb the ladder by climbing you."

I laugh. "Is that right?"

"Yes. It is. Please let me off the bar. I need to leave. Please, Grayson. I mean, Mr. Bennett."

I rotate us so that we're side by side, and she's no longer trapped, but my hands stay at her waist, hers on my chest when I want them all over my body. "Grayson," I say. "I hate Mr. Bennett. And I don't want you to leave, Mia. You interest me. I hope you're interested and not because of who I am."

"I am. I was, but how do I take that out of the equation?"

"I'm just a man."

"A billionaire."

"I'm just a man who wants to know you. Genuinely wants to know you and I can promise you that nothing between us will ever affect your job but neither does you walking away right now." I release her, but our legs are still touching and her hands don't leave my chest.

"I'm very confused right now." She leans back and her hands slide from my chest, but she doesn't step away. "I was interested in knowing you or I wouldn't have come here, but you being you, I need to think about this."

"I can live with that answer. Put my number in your phone. Then you can call me. You can decide what happens next."

"But you're my boss."

"Not directly. Let me have your phone."

She hesitates. I hate that she hesitates, but she reaches into her purse and hands me her phone. It rings and "Dad" comes up on her caller ID. "Sorry," she says and punches the decline button.

"You could have taken it," he says. "Fathers are important."

She tilts her head and studies me. "You're close to your father, too?"

"Very. As I was with my mother who I lost far too long ago."

She doesn't immediately respond and seems to weigh her words before she says, "I lost mine last year. I know it—it hurts. My dad is really struggling with it."

"Mine still does as well," I say, aware that it took my father well over a year to resemble anything I knew as him. "You should call your father back. You don't want him to worry."

"I'll call him in a few minutes. He knows I work long hours. See, that's just it. That's what I need you to know before I walk out of this bar. It's not because I want to. It's because I *have* to. I worked my way through school. I got accepted to two Ivy League colleges, but I couldn't go part-time or pay the tuition. I had to work for a tiny firm for two years to prove I can win cases just to get this job. And I can win. I was a good hire. I'll do a good job for you. And I can't blow that or risk being 'that' girl in the legal circles."

I let her story sink in. She could easily be someone who looks for a gravy train, but she's not and this isn't a show for her. She's not playing me. She's rejecting me, and I don't intend to let that happen. I'm still holding her phone and put my number in it, but I don't give it back to her. "I don't sleep with or date women my company employs."

"Why me?"

"You interest me, now more than ever." I cup her face. "I'm going to kiss you now unless you tell me to stop."

"I don't think you should do that."

"That's not stop, Mia."

"I know," she whispers, and my mouth closes down on hers, and the moment I taste her on my tongue, I know that I want more. And when she gives a tiny little whimper and leans into me, I know she does too, but still, I pull back and press her phone into her hand.

"You have my number. Call me, but know this, Mia. The next time I kiss you, I won't stop."

LISA RENEE JONES

CHAPTER THREE

Mia

The present

I don't stop in the foyer that is too small not to be too close to Grayson for comfort. I quickly clear the small space and enter the open concept living area with dark wood floors, high ceilings, and dangling lights. I stop there, on the edge of a living room that no longer looks as it once did, the black couches now replaced with gray leather that matches the kitchen island to the left. I swallow hard, thinking about how hard it must have been for Grayson to take over this place, let alone decide if he should leave it as it was or change it. He loved his father.

Grayson steps to my side and we both stare at the room and I wonder if he too is thinking about the funeral, and the last time we ever touched. The betrayal was gone that day, but the pain was not. "I won't say what I'm thinking," I say softly, my voice trembling ever-so-slightly.

"You don't have to. I know what you're thinking." He motions to the left. "Let's go downstairs."

Downstairs to the bar and entertainment area of the house. Downstairs, far away from the door. I wonder if he chooses this location to prevent my rapid escape, but nevertheless, this is his home. This is his decision. I nod and of course, he falls into step with me, but once we're at the winding gray and steel stairs leading downward, the path is made for one, and he does the gentlemanly thing and allows me to go first. I hesitate just a moment, but I start walking, grabbing the railing and carefully taking each step, aware of Grayson at my back in every pore of my body. Aware, too, that he didn't ask me why I'm here.

Once I'm on the lower level, there's a room with a brown sectional, a massive big-screen television to the left, and a fancy half-moon shaped bar to the right. "Let's drink," Grayson says, as he joins me, his shoulder brushing mine, and the touch is such a shock that I suck in air and cut my gaze.

I don't look at him, but I feel his stare before he moves toward the bar. I follow him, choosing a barstool opposite him as he rounds the oak countertop. "Still love your Brandy Alexanders?"

"Yes, but I better not. I'm driving back tonight. You know I don't handle my booze well." The reference to how well he knows me is out before I can stop it.

"I do know," he says, setting a glass in front of me before producing a bottle of brandy.

He then proceeds to mix my drink before filling his own glass with what I am certain is his favorite fifteen-year old scotch. He sets my glass in front of me. "But we both need a drink right about now." He picks up his glass, downs it, refills it, and then walks around the bar to stand beside me. So damn close that I can feel his body heat, and when my eyes meet his, I'm burning alive again, and yet I'm frozen in place.

"Grayson—"

"Grab your drink," he orders softly. "Let's go to the patio where you won't feel as trapped as you feel right now." He steps away from the bar and starts walking.

He knows me too well. He still knows me like no one else in this world, but it means nothing. Grayson observes people. He reads people. I pick up my drink and stand up. Grayson is to my left, opening the curtains. I join him as he opens the patio door and I step under the awning into the stone-encased private porch overlooking the ocean; the sun hidden behind clouds, a storm rumbling in the distance. I love storms over the ocean. The fireplace in the corner flickers to life and Grayson steps to my side.

I down my drink. "Now I can let it wear off before I drive." I set the glass on the table to our left that seats two and matches the one to our right, and then walk to the stone wall directly in front of us, my hands settling on the finished wooden rail above it.

I hear Grayson's glass touch the table before he steps to my side, his hands on the rail as well. "Talk to me, Mia."

I look over at him. "I came to warn you."

"What does that mean?"

"Ri is coming after you," I say.

He laughs. "Ri is always coming after me. He's been coming after me since law school when I made him look bad, and now that we both run our family empires, he's still trying to best me. He won when he got you."

I face him, and he does the same with me. "That's not even close to true. He didn't *get* me."

"He's my enemy and you left me, my bed and my company to go to him, his bed, and his company."

"That's not true. I needed a job and that's on *you*."

"You didn't need a damn job," he bites out.

I shove fingers through my hair. "This is not why I'm here. I need you to listen to me."

"You want to tell me how the man you're fucking wants to fuck me?"

"I am not fucking Ri. Stop. Listen to me, Grayson. *I need you* to *listen to me.*"

"Like you listened to me? Because I tried really damn hard to get you to listen to me, Mia. Do you remember? Because I damn sure do."

I hug myself, backing up to rest against the concrete pillar behind me. "I listened. It wasn't enough, but you need to listen to me now. I just took a week off to look for a new job. I went to an interview at the DA's office."

"The DA's office? You won't make any money there. Why would you consider it? You're too good for that place."

"I'm tired of money. Your money. Ri's money. I want to be someplace that wasn't about money and power, only I was there all of forty-five minutes and I knew that place was no different. They're all looking for power, the kind you have, which makes them hate you."

"What does that mean?"

"I was sitting in an office with an open door. There were men, four of them, I think, in the conference room across from me. They were talking about the billionaire who pretends to be ethical and perfect. Who thinks he's untouchable, but he's not. They said they have insiders in your operation. They said they're going to take you down and look like kings."

"Did they say my name?"

"No, but—"

"I don't break the law. That's not me."

"I know that. That's why I'm here. I was afraid your phones were being monitored because Grayson, it was you they were talking about. I know it. I felt it and I remember a card from a detective on Ri's desk. He's somehow setting you up."

He narrows his eyes at me. "And you're telling me, the man you say betrayed you, why?"

"You're not a criminal. And that's all I have to say." I push off the wall and try to walk past Grayson, but he shackles my arm and pulls me to him.

We stare at each other, our lower bodies pressed together, the past between us, and in this moment, it's pulling us closer, not pushing us apart. Thunder crashes above us and rain explodes from the sky, plummeting the ceiling above us and beyond the patio. Grayson tangles the fingers of one hand in my hair, while the other flattens between my shoulder blades. "You didn't really think I'd let you leave without doing this, did you?" he asks, his mouth closing down on mine.

CHAPTER FOUR

Mia

The minute Grayson's mouth is on my mouth, his body pressed to mine, I forget everything but him. It's like I can breathe again, like I've barely been living until right here, right now. I don't want to, but I still love him, and I didn't think I would ever kiss him or touch him again. He backs me up and presses me against the wide concrete pillar that divides the railings and walls, his fingers tangling into my hair, his hand slipping under my sweater, his warm palm pressing to my ribcage. It's not until that hand cups my breast that I jolt into reality.

"Stop," I say, catching his hand and pressing on his chest. "Stop. I can't do this."

He goes still but he doesn't immediately release me. God, I don't want him to release me and yet, I cannot survive the onslaught of emotions he creates in me if I don't stop now. I can't just fuck him. It's not in me. "Right," he says, his hand falling away, and pressing onto the concrete on either side of me, his body lifting away from mine. "You're with Ri."

"I'm not with Ri, and if I was with him or anyone, it wouldn't be any of your business. We're not together anymore."

"You went from me to him; you went to my enemy. Do you know how badly that cut? That's when I stopped coming after you. That's when I let you go."

"I was trying to survive. You were cut? I was bleeding out. And do you really think I'd come to you if I was with Ri? I'm a loyal person. I never betrayed you. I wouldn't betray someone I was with."

"Unlike me, right?" he challenges. "I did not betray you. I've tried to explain."

"I'm not here to talk about this. I can't go down this path again. It still hurts and me telling you that is more than you deserve."

He stares at me, those green eyes unreadable, but his emotions are radiating off of him and pounding on me even as the rain pounds against the roof. He pushes off the pillar and walks a foot away to plant his hand on the railing and lowers his chin to his chest.

I can still feel his hand on my breast. I can still taste him and it's killing me. "I said what I came to say. I should go." But I don't move. I don't push off the pillar.

"Don't," he says, looking over at me. "Don't go."

There's torment in his voice, a guttural plea that conflicts with all he did to me. I know this, but I don't move. I squeeze my eyes shut. "I don't know why I'm still standing here." My lashes lift. "I can't stay. I have to go." I move then, I try to walk past him, but he pushes off the railing and steps in front of me.

"Eric and Davis are about to be here," he says of his best friend and business manager, and his personal attorney. "I'd like them to hear what you had to say."

"You can tell them."

"I'd like them to hear it from you."

"I need to get back."

"Stay the night and you can chopper back with me tomorrow."

"I have a rental car," I argue.

"I'll take care of it for you."

I hug myself. "I don't need or want you to take care of anything for me."

He looks skyward and then lowers his head to cast me in a turbulent stare. "You're helping me. It's the least I can do."

I inhale and let it out. "I'll get a room and drive back tomorrow."

"This house is ridiculously large. You can stay on another floor. You'll never know I'm here."

"I'll know you're here." I turn away from him and press my hands to the railing. He mimics my action and we stand there, side by side, the rain pounding fiercely.

"You always loved the rain on the ocean," he murmurs after a few moments.

I loved it when I was with him. I have good memories of loving it *with* him. "I won't let you hurt me again," I whisper.

We look at each other, a punch in the connection between us before he says, "I never meant to hurt you. I would die for you, Mia. That hasn't changed."

I cut my stare, so very confused because I believe him and that makes the way we ended illogical, at least for me, at least for my way of loving someone. I don't understand his kind of love and yet I need it so damn badly. "If I'm staying, I'll take a glass of that scotch."

I feel his eyes on me, those perfect, intelligent green eyes, before he says, "Scotch it is," and pushes off the railing. "I'll be right back."

I nod, but I don't watch him walk away. I stare out into the rain and my mind goes back to another day, back to the

25

funeral, to sitting in the car and staring at the church. I hadn't seen Grayson in six painful months. I'd told myself that I was out of his life. I'd told myself that he wouldn't want me there, but I'd cared about his father and I still loved him. And so, I'd gotten out of that car. I'd gone inside.

Grayson's footsteps sound behind me and I turn as he sets the bottle down on a table between the two chairs facing the fireplace. He fills two glasses, mine with ice, and his without because he knows I'll want ice, and then he hands me mine. I know he's going to touch me, but I don't resist. I reach for my glass and when our hands collide, he catches mine and walks me to him.

Heat radiates up my arm from where he touches me and I know if I look at him, I'll forget why that kiss was bad when it felt so damn good. For several seconds we just stand there, rain and history suffocating us until he reaches up and brushes my cheek. The touch shocks me, and I shiver, my gaze jerking to his. "Let's sit down by the fire," he says softly.

"I'd like that."

He seems to hesitate to release my hand, but it slowly slides away and neither of us move. The wind gushes and that's enough to set us in motion. I walk around the chairs and sit down in front of the fire, sipping from the glass. "That's strong," I say as he sits down next to me and I place the glass on the table between us. "Maybe you need to drink mine. Eric and Davis aren't going to be an easy audience for me." I lean forward and hold my hands toward the fire, my elbows on my knees.

Grayson leans forward with me, only he ignores the fire. "They've both always liked you, Mia. You know that."

"They're your friends, your very good friends. They'll protect you, which is good. That's why I came. So you can throw up the armor."

"I thought I had," he says. "And then you showed up at my door." Grayson's cellphone buzzes with a text, and he pulls it from his pocket, glancing at the screen. "Eric," he says. "They're almost here." He sticks his cell back into his pocket, downs his drink, and stands up. "Let's meet them upstairs."

I nod and decide I do need that drink. I pick it up and take a big slug before setting it down. I stand up and turn to walk toward the door but Grayson steps in front of me. "Don't even think about leaving while they're here. I'll come after you, and this time I won't stop coming." He pulls me to him, his long legs pressed to mine. "We're not done, Mia. Not now. Not tonight. Not ever. We're done pretending otherwise." He kisses me, a brush of lips over lips that I feel in every part of me before he rotates us and turns me to the door, his hands on my shoulders, my back to his front as he leans in and whispers, "But be warned. I'm not going to stop the next time I kiss you."

CHAPTER FIVE

Mia

Grayson's warning twists me in knots and ultimately anger takes root. I whirl around to face him. "You don't get to say what we do or don't do. You don't get to decide if we kiss or not. You don't get to decide if we start or stop. You're not in control anymore."

"I was never in control," he says, his voice tight with returned anger. "Not with you."

"Are you kidding me? You controlled everything in the past. I was making my first real career move and your father—you, basically—owned the company. You had money and power and I came from nothing. You were this force of nature I wanted to be near. I wanted to learn from you. I wanted to be with you. You consumed me. I—this is not then. You're not in control this time."

His hands come down on my arms and he pulls me to him. "It sure as hell didn't feel like I was in control when you left, and I bled out both times, Mia. Both fucking times."

Both times.

He means after the funeral, which is just another knife in my chest.

"Look at us," I say. "This is who we are, Grayson. Pain and anger. Why would you want to keep me here?"

The doorbell rings and he curses, but he doesn't let me go. "Because the pain and anger are about a betrayal that never fucking happened." He tangles his fingers in my hair. "We have never fought this out honestly and completely. And because of this." His mouth closes down on mine, his tongue stroking deep, and every part of me inside and out, melts into him, into us, when I don't mean to. The doorbell rings again and he tears his mouth from mine. "We're still us. We're *still us*."

"I don't know what that means anymore."

"You will," he promises, his hands coming down on my arms once more. "Mia—"

The doorbell rings again and he grimaces. "Damn it. They aren't going away. I have to let them in."

"You do," I say. "We need to talk with them about Ri."

"Ri," he repeats tightly. "Yes. Let's talk about Ri." He releases me, a cold snap in the air as he motions me forward.

I don't like this reaction. I don't like what he thinks is between Ri and I, but I decide maybe it works right now, especially where Ri is concerned. He needs to find that hard, cold part of himself and find it now. He needs to focus on the war before him, not on me, not on us. With that thought, I launch myself across the room, hurrying up the stairs, and I half expect his hand on mine at any moment, but it doesn't happen. I've hit a nerve in him and some part of me revels in the fact that he has nerves to be hit. If he didn't care about me, he wouldn't, but I don't know why it matters. I don't want to do love his way.

I reach the upper level and I decide to offer Grayson privacy with his team to explain why I'm here, and I do so without his permission. I cross the living room and head out to the upstairs patio that oversees a rectangular infinity pool that seems to flow right into the ocean when it doesn't. I flip on the heater and ignore the round table that he often uses for meetings. Instead, I stand at the railing overlooking the pool, watching the now steady, but slower flow of raindrops hit its surface.

"Mia."

At the sound of Eric's voice, I turn to find him joining me, his light brown hair tousled, his blue eyes as intelligent as ever, but then why wouldn't they be? This is a man who's been by Grayson's side, helping him make billions, for damn near a decade. "Hi, Eric," I say, hugging myself.

"It's been a long time," he says, setting his briefcase on the table, while his snug black tee allows me a clear view of his tattoo sleeve that was once a lion with blue eyes, and now travels down his arm in a collage of clocks and skulls. "I haven't seen you since—" He stops himself, his lips thinning.

"The funeral," I supply. "I can't believe that's been a year now."

"I know," he says. "I can't either. I don't know how the hell Grayson lives in this place, aside from the fact that he's in the city so damn much." He shakes his head. "Enough of that, though. Davis needed Grayson to call an investor. They'll be right here."

"Good. I'm glad to have a moment with you. Maybe you'll listen before they get here because I'm not sure Grayson will. He's in trouble."

"If you're here, then he must be." He closes the space between us. "Talk to me."

"I'll tell you what I've told him." I tell him everything, the job, the interview, what I overheard at the DA's office. "They were talking about Grayson. I know they were and I saw that card on Ri's desk. Please tell me that you see that as the problem I do."

He narrows his eyes at me. "Why are you here if you're with Ri?"

"I'm not with Ri, and I'm smart enough to see the writing on the wall. He wants me to taunt Grayson. I'm a token in a game."

"And yet you went to him."

"I took a job, and I'm certain you know more about why than maybe I did before—" I stop myself. "At the time, I admit I was angry at Grayson and hurt. I just needed a place to go."

"You knew how he'd feel about you going to Ri."

"Do you know how I felt about what *he* did?" I hold up a hand. "It doesn't matter. I'm not with Ri and I'm tired of being a token in a game between two powerful men."

"You're not a token," Eric says. "You're the woman Grayson loves and that hasn't changed. You're a weapon Ri is using against him."

"I know that now," I say. "That's why I'm here. I'm not going to be a weapon against Grayson. Not now or ever."

Grayson steps onto the porch and our eyes meet, the charge between us cracking. "I never intended to be a weapon against you, Grayson. Please believe that."

Grayson lowers his lashes, the lines of his face hard and sharp. He's struggling to maintain control, and he never struggles to maintain control, because of me. Because we both know I'm not completely innocent. I did leave him and go to his enemy. I did know that would upset him. I wanted to hurt him the way he hurt me.

"I regret it," I breathe out, saying the words I should have said a long time ago, the words I'd rather say to him alone. "I regret going to him, Grayson."

His lashes lift and I don't find forgiveness or understanding. I find anger.

CHAPTER SIX

Mia

"Mia," Davis says, stepping to Grayson's side; he's a tall man, in his late thirties, with dark brown hair and a beard to match. Today he's left his famously expensive suits behind for jeans and a T-shirt. "It's been a long time," he says warmly when he's rarely warm to anyone. "*Too long.*"

I am stunned by how warm his greeting is and this tells me that Grayson never gave him reason to hate me. He's angry, yes. They know he's angry, but my stomach twists with the idea that they're sympathetic to me, that they know he's guilty of *much* with me. Some part of me wants to believe he's not. I've always wanted to believe that he's not, perhaps because I had this fairytale idea of who and what we could be, what I thought we were. Maybe because my father loved my mother to the point of no return. He would have died for her. The man gave her part of his lung to try to save her life. And no, it's not a fairytale in that she died, but their love was.

Now *my* lashes lower, the pain of losing Grayson is acid in my throat. "Let's sit," Grayson says, motioning to the table, and we all listen because he's the one in charge, and not because this is his house. Because no matter how powerful the people in the room, Grayson owns the room

33

itself, he's in control and I've always found this incredibly alluring. What I didn't do, was fear where that would lead me or what that power over me meant until he burned me. I cannot allow him to burn me again.

I walk to the table and sit down, noting the rain has now stopped, the only storm left is that between myself and Grayson. Eric sits to my right, Davis across from me, but there is only one person that consumes me. Grayson sits to my left and when we look at each other, no one else exists, a million unspoken words and so much anger between us.

Eric clears his throat. "I'll update Davis. Grayson, Mia ran through the situation with me. To make a long story short, Mia was at the DA's office for an interview."

"An interview?" Davis asks. "Why the fuck would you interview with the DA?"

"Irrelevant," Eric states. "She overheard a plan to take down Grayson."

"Grayson doesn't break the law," Davis states. "This is ridiculous."

"It's a set-up," I say. "I saw one of the detective's cards on Ri's desk. I think he's behind it all and that means he's doing what he has to in order to ensure Grayson looks guilty."

Grayson looks at Eric. "Where are we weak enough to allow this to happen?"

"You have employees worldwide, Grayson," he says. "Anyone could be paid off to plant false information, or to even go so far as to break the law. I told you. We should have dealt with Ri years ago."

"He had Mia," Grayson says. "I didn't think he'd act beyond that, but obviously, that's changed."

"I know a guy at the DA's office," Davis says. "I'll make a call. It'll cost us, but he'll get us what we need to know. If he confirms there's a problem, we're at war and we need a good criminal attorney advising us. I'm corporate and I'm good, but I want an expert in here."

"I'm criminal law," Grayson says. "I can handle it. I don't want anyone involved that could leak this."

"You haven't actively practiced in years," Eric argues. "And you're too close to this personally. I agree with Davis. We'll need an expert to help you insulate yourself."

"I'm a criminal lawyer," I say. "I'm actively practicing and I'm good at my job."

"You're too close to this, *and* to the enemy," Davis says, his voice hard now.

"I haven't lost a case," I say, that topic hitting a nerve between Grayson and I that has me avoiding his stare. "And I haven't resigned from Ri's company. I can get close to him and—"

Grayson gives a bitter laugh. "That's priceless, Mia. Really fucking priceless. You left me to fuck him and now you want to fuck him for me? Or fuck him because you aren't fucking me anymore." He stands up and without a word, walks into the house.

My emotions quake inside me and I can feel my hands shaking when I never shake, but this is Grayson. This is the man I still love and never stopped loving. I look between the two men he trusts the most. "I'm not with Ri. I have never been with Ri. I swear to you both."

"He's the one who needs to hear it," Eric says. "Not us."

He's right.

I stand up and follow Grayson, shutting the sliding glass door as I enter the living room.

I find him behind the island, his hand on the counter, head dipped low, my regret I'd declared gnawing at me. I'm not a person that lashes back. I really didn't lash back the way he thinks I lashed back, and for reasons he might not deserve, I really need him to know the truth. I don't leave the island between us. I round the counter and I stand beside him, facing the counter, not him.

"I've never been with Ri. I know you think I was, but I haven't been. He's tried for years. Recently I was lonely. I was *really* lonely, Grayson. I saw a picture of you with a woman and I realized that you'd moved on and I hadn't."

"I didn't fucking move on, Mia," he says turning to face me. "I was trying to survive you fucking my enemy."

I whirl around to face him as well. "I didn't, though. I didn't fuck Ri." My voice lifts as I add, "*Ever.* After seeing you with her, I finally agreed to go out with him. I tried to do what you think I already did and I had to drink wine, lots of wine, to try and actually make it happen. I mean, why wouldn't I? You and I—and you were—" I stop myself. "It doesn't matter why. I had too much wine. I fell asleep on his couch and even after seeing you with that woman, I dreamed about you, and us, and I called out your name."

"You did what?"

"I called out your name and since I was dreaming about the funeral, after the funeral, actually, the last time we were together, it wasn't in anger, but passion."

He's still, so very still, before he says, "And what did he do?"

"He was furious and then he grabbed me and tried to force himself on me. He told me he'd make me forget you."

Grayson's hands come down on my arms and he pulls me to him. "Did he force himself on you? Because if he did, I'll kill him."

He speaks those words with such guttural anger that I believe him. My hand settles on his chest, his heart racing beneath my palm. "I gave him a knee so damn hard, I doubt he walked right for a week."

"I'm not sure that's a good enough punishment."

"He didn't touch me again. He got the point. Grayson, I should never have gone to him at all. He wanted what was yours and I knew that and even though he couldn't have me, at least, to him, you thought he did. Now, I left him and he's lashing out. I did this. I did this to you and I'm so sorry. You have to let me help. I don't want to go near that man, but I need you to understand that I'll do it for you."

He tangles his fingers into my hair. "Going back to him is like sticking another knife in my heart, Mia. You will not go back to him. Do you understand me?"

"If it protects you, I will."

"You will not. That's not up for debate."

"You don't get to decide."

He turns me and pins me between himself and the counter, his powerful legs caging mine, his hands on my waist. "On this," he says. "Watch me. I'm not letting you go back to him. Even if I have to do what I should have done before and tie you to my damn bed until you listen to reason. One of my biggest regrets is not doing that a year ago, so I damn sure will do it now."

CHAPTER SEVEN

Mia

"Grayson—" I say, determined to make him listen.

"Don't," he says. "I know you still know that look and that plea on your lips makes me give in, but not this time. Not when it comes to you and Ri."

"I'm here because I caused this, because I care. You don't have to tie me to your bed. I'm staying. I'm not leaving. Please, just tell me you'll hear me out."

"Quid pro quo. I hear you out. You hear me out."

We're going down this path of the past. I can't stop it from happening. I'm not sure, if I'm honest with myself or him, that I want to stop it. "On one condition. We deal with us after him because I don't want either of us letting the past get in the way of shutting Ri down."

"Then we operate just like we did at the funeral. Nothing is off limits."

"Grayson—"

He cups my face and kisses me, a deep slide of tongue that has me biting back a moan. "God, I missed kissing you."

I missed it too, so very much, but I don't say that to him. I can't.

He rests his forehead against mine. "I need to go talk to Eric and Davis."

"Yes," I agree, pressing on his chest and forcing him to look at me, "you do. Be open-minded to what they say. I want to help."

"You have. You've motivated me to destroy him once and for all."

His voice is hard, the glint in his eye pure evil genius that actually comforts me. You don't beat Grayson Bennett when he's in this state of mind, but that also means he won't listen to reason on my influence over Ri. "I just packaged a convention center deal in Japan. There are a few legal issues on that project that are time-sensitive. I have to deal with that today. I have no choice."

"A convention center. Wow. That's huge."

"It is. It's going to double our worth."

And make Ri hate him all the more. "I'm not going anywhere, Grayson. Take care of your business. Just make sure Ri is part of that business."

He presses his hands on the island on either side of me. "You didn't cause his attack, Mia. I did. I let this misunderstanding between us go on too long, but no more." He pushes off the counter. "Do you have a bag in the car?"

"Yes. I was afraid I couldn't get to you tonight."

He studies me a long moment. "I'll get your bag." He starts to move away.

I catch his arm. "It's light. I'll get it. You go take care of business."

"Take it to my room. That's part of the deal. We put the past on hold."

My lashes lower and he cups my face. "Mia. Look at me."

I open my eyes. "My room," he says.

"Yes," I say, finding the idea that I would pretend I'd end up anywhere else a waste of energy at this point that would border on the kind of games I don't like to play. "Your room. I'm going to take a walk, though. I need to clear my head. I'll take my phone. You know my number."

His hand comes down on the island beside me again. "Yes. I know your number, just like you know the gate code to this house when no one else does. There was *never* a time when you couldn't get to me, Mia. You just didn't choose to find out until now." There is anger in his words again, in his voice. He pushes off the island and walks away and that anger is what I focus on.

He's angry, like I betrayed him, and for the first time since right after the funeral, I let myself consider the option that he's not guilty of at least one of his sins, the unforgivable one, but I shove that naiveté away. I know what happened. I swallow hard and quickly push off the island and start walking, my path leading me to my car, where I open the trunk and remove a hoodie from my suitcase. I pull it on and then head down a walkway at the side of the house that leads to the beach. Once I'm there, I walk to the edge of the water and turn and stare at the house.

This was his father's place, but we were here more weekends than his father. This is where we came after the funeral. This was where our final goodbye took place. Memories of that day charge at me and I turn away from the house and start running, the way I used to run this beach. I don't stop until I'm two miles away at the lighthouse, which I didn't just come to with Grayson. He'd bought it because I loved it so much. The sun is dimming, soon to begin fading into the horizon, the way Grayson and I faded into the horizon.

I start climbing the winding steps until I'm at the very top where Grayson and I had set-up cozy reclining chairs, side by side. I claim the one that was mine, and I painfully wonder if any other woman has been here with Grayson when I have no right. We aren't together. We haven't been together in a long time. I pull my knees to my chest and I think of his father, who is now gone. I think of the funeral, as I have so many times since he left this world. The way I did the night I pissed off Ri. It was almost a new beginning until Grayson left his phone on the bed, and I saw the number on his phone.

Grayson

I'm not a man who builds his success on other people's destruction, but I have limits, and Ri is going to find out that he's pushed me too far. I walk out onto the patio and sit down with Eric and Davis. "Go," I say, which is what I use as an invitation for them to hit me with their thoughts, of which I'm certain they have many after hearing Mia's reasons for being here.

"She's always had good instincts," Eric says. "If she believes that conversation was about you, I'm betting on her."

"Agreed," Davis says. "I trust her, and I don't trust anyone. I still think we need a criminal attorney in on this."

"What we need," I say, "is an attack plan. I want Ri to go down once and for all. Make that happen and I don't care what resources, including money, it takes. Pay whoever, as much money as you have to pay them, to get the right dirt on him, to shut him down."

"Mia's already on the inside," Davis says. "She—"

"No," I say. "Mia will not go back to Ri. End of subject. What else do I need to know right here and now?"

"Reid and Carrie are headed back to Japan to take care of the challenges with the convention center takeover," Eric says, of the brokers who brought the deal together. "The other ten things on my list can wait." He eyes Davis. "We need a minute."

Davis gives him a nod and stands up. Eric waits until Davis enters the house and then leans closer. "I don't know what happened between you and Mia, but not only did it change you, it clearly hurt her. Despite that, she was there for you when your father died and she is here now. Considering the pain I still see in her eyes, I know two things: a) she still loves you, and b) she believes this threat is serious."

"I'm not discounting the threat, Eric. I said ruin him."

"You have thousands of employees, including me, counting on you. You don't have the luxury of leaving her out of this."

"Find another way," I order.

"Protect her, but keep an open mind. She could be the only person who can tear him down."

"Find another way," I repeat, and this time I stand up. "I will not have her feel as if I'm using her for my own gain or that I'm putting my well-being over hers."

He stands. "Not yours. Thousands of employees."

"And I damn sure won't risk hurting her again," I add as if he hasn't spoken. "I love you, man, and you're the brother I never had, but don't push me on this. Not on Mia." I step away from the table and head for the walkway down to the beach, with one destination in mind. The lighthouse, where I know Mia will be right now.

CHAPTER EIGHT

Mia

The past, six months ago

I pull up to the curb a few blocks from the Hamptons church and park the rental I picked up to get here from the city since I don't own a car that I'd never drive anyway. No one owns a car in Manhattan who doesn't have parking money to blow, and after growing up in a poor area of Brooklyn, I'm pretty sure I'll never feel I have that kind of money to blow. It's why I declined the car Grayson tried to buy me way back when. I didn't need it and his money was never what we were about to me. I always wanted him to know that. I always felt he *needed* to know that.

I breathe a heavy breath and kill the engine, my hands gripping the steering wheel. I want to be here for Grayson, no matter what has transpired between Grayson and I, but I don't know if I'm making this pain better or worse for him. I still love him. I don't want to make it worse, but this was not expected. A heart attack is never expected. I need Grayson to know that I wanted to be here, even if he rejects me. Even if he has someone else by his side now.

I swallow against the dryness in my throat and step out of the car, slipping the slender black purse I'm wearing over my black dress, across my chest. I shove the door

45

shut, and damn it, my knees are wobbling. I push forward and start walking, along with a good ten other people parked nearby. I can feel eyes on me, surprised eyes that know I was with Grayson and I'm not anymore, but I don't care. I'm not here for them.

Once I reach the gorgeous white church, which ironically has three steeples just like Grayson's father's house just down the road does, I stand on the sidewalk and just stare at the door. It's almost time for the service and there are no people lingering here or there, as I'm certain there would have been earlier. I make my way up the concrete path and then travel a good twenty steps. I enter the church, and as soon as I'm inside, Eric, dressed in a black suit, is standing in front of me, as if he'd seen me approach.

"Did he tell you to send me away?"

"No," he says. "He doesn't know you're here, but he won't send you away. He needs you."

My eyes are already starting to burn. "Take me to him," I whisper.

He motions to the left, and I follow him down a hallway to a doorway where we stop. "He's alone."

I nod and he opens the door. I inhale and shut my eyes, deep breathing for a few beats. I haven't seen Grayson in six months which feel like a century. I have so many hurt feelings with him but now is not about those feelings. I open my eyes and enter a compact prayer room to find Grayson standing in front of a cross with his back to me.

"Grayson," I say softly.

His shoulders flex, his entire body tensing before he slowly turns to face me and even today, in a black pinstriped suit, his face etched in grief for a father he loved dearly, he is beautiful. "Mia," he breathes out as if he's seeing an illusion.

"Yes. I—I wanted to be here for you and him. I hope it's okay. If it's not—"

He's across the room in a matter of two blinks and pulling me to into his arms, his hand cupping my head, his mouth closing down on mine, and I'm consumed by his grief and need, by his hunger for something that is both physical and emotional. There is no part of me that holds back. No part of me that doesn't want to give him what he needs.

"Don't leave," he whispers. "I need you."

"I'm not going anywhere," I say. "I'm right here. I wanted to call sooner. I just didn't know if I would make it worse."

"I need you," is all he says, his forehead resting against mine, and he doesn't speak or move.

We just stand there holding each other, time ticking by—seconds, minutes, I'm not sure how long—until Grayson breaks the silence.

"I golfed with him that morning. I was there when it happened. I couldn't save him."

I pull back to look at him and there are tears in his eyes. I reach up and stroke away the dampness on his cheeks, more in love with this man in this moment than I ever have been. He is strong, powerful, and wealthy, and yet, he is human, he is vulnerable. "Did you get to tell him you love him?"

"Yes. Over and over. I'm not sure he heard, though."

"He knew. *He knew.*"

The door opens and Eric says, "It's time."

Grayson pulls back and looks at him. "We'll be right there."

Eric nods and exits. Grayson takes my hand. "I'm giving the eulogy."

"As it should be," I say.

He bends our elbows and pulls me close, his eyes meeting mine. "As it should be," he says. He's talking about me by his side.

"Yes," I say, without hesitation. "As it should be."

He brings our joined hands to his lips and kisses them before he guides me forward and we exit the room. Hand in hand, we enter the church, which is packed with hundreds of people and we walk down the center aisle with all eyes on us. We sit in the front row, and Leslie, his godmother, his second mother, who was his mother's best friend, reaches around and squeezes my leg, her long dark hair pulled back at the nape, her blue eyes pained. I realize then that Grayson is alone but for her. His mother has been gone for five years. Now his father is gone as well.

Grayson doesn't let go of me until it's his turn to speak. He looks at me when it's time and I cup his face. "As it should be," I whisper, and he kisses me before he stands.

I listen to the heartfelt words about a man who inspired him, a man who was hard on him, but only because he wanted the best for him, and every word is true. "He was a hard man who expected honesty and ethics. He expected that I be the best and I do it with hard work and integrity."

When Grayson is done there isn't a dry eye in the church and the minute he's seated again, he's holding onto me, his grip so tight it hurts, but I don't care. The rest of the ceremony is over quickly and it's not long before I'm in the front seat of Grayson's Porsche for the ride to the cemetery. He cranks the engine but doesn't place us in gear. "It was perfect," I whisper when we're finally alone. "And true. He was a good man."

"He asked me every time I saw him when you'd be back." He looks at me, his green eyes bloodshot. "Every time, Mia. For six months."

"I'm here now," I whisper. "I'm not leaving."

I mean it when I say it. I never wanted to leave in the first place.

He reaches for me, his fingers tangling in my hair. "We're going to the house," he says. "Do you have a problem with that?"

"On one condition," I say, my hand covering his. "We don't talk about why I left. I don't want to talk about it. I just want us to be us right now."

"We never stopped being us, Mia," he says, pulling my mouth to his and kissing me. And in that kiss, I taste the truth. He's right. We never stopped being us and while I've questioned if I knew what that meant over the past few months, I don't now. Right now, us, is what it always was before: everything.

CHAPTER NINE

Mia

The present

I come back to the present, back to the retired lighthouse Grayson bought to please me, back to my present location of the cozy chair we'd picked out together, but I'm not really here. I'm not fully outside the memory of the funeral, and I'm as confused as I was that weekend. When he'd seen me at the church, when he'd pulled me to him, I'd thought I'd been wrong to leave him. I'd thought I was wrong about so much and that I belonged with him.

And then there was the text message.

The message that made me leave again. The message that told me that he would always hurt me, but one look into his eyes, one touch of his hand, and I'd believed we were real and pure again. Like I do now. What am I thinking, being here? What am I trying to do to myself?

I stand up and rush toward the stairs as Grayson appears in front of me, so damn good looking, so damn perfect in so many ways. His hands settle on my waist, branding me. His touch, his presence, always claims me, even when I don't want to want to be claimed. And yet I always do with him. Right now, I'm lost, that familiar, woodsy, delicious scent of him mixing with the ocean air and consuming me as easily as the man himself. "Looking for me?" he asks softly, backing me up until I'm pressed to the bright blue wall of the lighthouse, a color we chose together. We did so many things together, everything together. He was my life, my love, my best friend.

I thought.

I flatten my hands on his chest, hard muscle beneath my palms, and I intend to push him away, but instead, my palms settle there, they feel as if they belong there; the ease at which I touch him, defying our breakup and his betrayal. "Your meeting was short, too short. What are you doing about Ri?"

He studies me, those green eyes far too intelligent for my own good. "You were about to run again, weren't you?"

"I never ran," I correct him. "Leaving and running are two different things. I made a decision. If I leave now, it's another decision."

"A decision to leave me over a lie someone else set up." He releases me and presses his hands to the wall, no longer touching me. "Obviously there's a bigger picture here. If there wasn't, you wouldn't have believed the lie."

"Lie? Regardless of the portions of this that you call a lie, there was more to me leaving, and you know it." I curl my fingers on his chest. "I said I didn't want to talk about this."

"Just like you didn't want to talk about it at the funeral?"

"Your father had just died, Grayson. I wasn't selfish enough to make that about me. I cared about your father. I still loved you."

"Loved?"

"If I didn't still love you, do you think I'd really be here?"

He stares at me, his eyes suddenly hard. "Then why the fuck were you with Ri?" he demands, his voice low, hard, affected.

He pushes off the wall and turns away, walking to the half wall encasing the private sitting area, his shoulders bunched beneath his T-shirt. I inhale with the bitterness in his words and the pain beneath them. He hurt me, but I hurt him back and I don't like that about me. It's my turn to push off the wall. I close the space between us, and once again we're side by side, facing the ocean, both of us gripping a railing when we could so easily be touching each other, too easily, and yet, not easy enough.

"I should never have gone to work for Ri's company. I regret it. I'm sorry."

We look at each other. "You were trying to hurt me. It worked."

"No. No, I never wanted to hurt you." I turn to face him, but he doesn't face me. "I've thought a lot about this in the last twenty-four hours, especially on the drive up here. I asked myself if I went to Ri to hurt you, but I didn't. I didn't want to hurt you. I was trying to survive."

Now he rotates to face me. "By going to him? By leaving my bed, not once but twice, and going to *him*?"

"I didn't sleep with him. Ever. And I didn't want to hurt you. I was desperate for a place to shelter that you didn't own, and Ri's world was the only place I knew you didn't own."

"You wanted away from me that damn badly?"

"No. I wanted to go back to you that badly and Ri's world was the only world that made that unacceptable. It was the only place I was strong enough to just say no, but I see now that I made a mistake. I opened the door for him to go after you. Why are you here, and not talking to Eric and Davis about Ri? You *need* to deal with him. *We* need to deal with him."

"*We?* That's a loaded word."

"I'm here for a reason," I say. "I want to help."

"You told me. I'm handling it."

"What does that even mean?" I press.

"It means that I don't go after many people, but he's pushed my limits." His jaw sets, hard. "You need to know that I plan to hurt him. I plan to make sure he can't come for me, or you, again and that's not on you any more than his actions are on you."

"If you expect me to tell you not to hurt him, if this is a test of loyalty to you or him, I'm not failing that test. Because we both know it is. You *need* to hurt him because he will destroy you if he can. I've seen how he works. He's not you."

"Did you think he was? Did you think he could be?"

"Never, Grayson. I told you. I wasn't with him."

"But you went out with him."

"Long after we broke up and yet, I still said your name when I was with him. I told you. I was alone. I was alone and—"

He shackles my waist and pulls me to him, the heat of his body enveloping mine. "You didn't have to be alone. You were never supposed to be alone and neither was I."

"You're never alone."

"I am always alone without you." His forehead lowers to mine. "I stood in that church and willed you to appear." He pulls back to look at me, his hand sliding under my hair. "I couldn't breathe until you were there. That's how much a part of me you are." His lips brush mine, a feather-light touch I feel in every part of me before they part mine. We linger there a moment, breathing together, the way we haven't in so very long. "You have to feel how much I need you," he whispers, his hands sliding between my shoulder blades.

How much I need him, I think. "I'm still angry."

"I'm angry with you, too," he says, and his mouth comes down on mine, with his promise that the next time he kisses me he won't stop in the air between us but it doesn't matter.

Right now is just like after the funeral. We're here. We're alone. I have been so alone without him and I don't want to think about the past. I want to think about the here and now and him. The muscles low in my belly clench. My nipples ache. My heart melts. He turns me and presses me against the wall of the lighthouse in a small alcove between the stairs and the cutout view.

He reaches for the zipper of my hoodie and the lick of his tongue consumes me. I moan into his mouth and somehow his hand has caressed up my sweater to cup my breast. I gasp and arch into the touch, but a rumble of thunder shocks me, pulling me back to reality. I grab Grayson's hand. "Wait. Wait. Not here." I press on his chest and when he pulls back just enough to look at me, I add, "This place is special and not for one reason. I don't want to be here with you when we're like we are now."

"It *is* special, which is exactly why we need to be here, to remember who we are together. I know you don't want to talk now, but we have to talk. It's time, Mia. It's past time."

"I know," I concede, "but not before we—not tonight. I don't want to need to leave again. And I don't want this place to become about a final goodbye."

His lashes lower and he cuts his gaze, torment etched in his handsome face before he looks at me again. "Be clear, Mia," he says softly. "We will not part ways in the middle again. I want you. I *will* fight for you, but we're in or we're out. We're together or we both move on once and for all."

CHAPTER TEN

Mia

The past, a year and three months ago

The sky and the ocean are the same blue today, I think, my hands resting on the ledge of the cutout inside the lighthouse that sits a couple of miles down from Grayson's family home. So blue, so perfect that despite the sky and the ocean starting at different places, they meld together as one. The way I do with Grayson. I rotate and rest my elbows on the ledge, my gaze landing on Grayson where he sits in one of the cozy chairs we picked out recently for our many hours spent here. His gaze is downturned, focused on his MacBook as he goes over numbers on the newest of his nationwide expansion of his father's law firm, this one opening in Washington. He's so damn good looking, so unassuming in faded jeans and a black snug T-shirt that hugs his impressive chest, his dark wavy hair rumpled and not from the wind. Because I can't ever keep my fingers out of it.

He glances up and his green eyes meet mine, and even after nine months and almost every day since with him, I feel the punch of that connection. I feel him in every part of me. He winks the way he does often like we're sharing a private secret, which we often do, and I smile, reaching for my wine glass on the table beside him. He catches my hand and pulls me to him, kissing me before he scowls into the phone. "Negative, Eric," he says, and then releases me. "I do not like the numbers on that building. Tell Davis if he can't negotiate better than that, I'll do it myself."

My lips curve because Davis, like Eric, is one of Grayson's closest friends, but Grayson doesn't pull any punches with them. When it comes to business, he's smart, savvy, and if need be, brutal but he's always honest. The honest part is probably the thing that makes me love him beyond all else, and there is plenty of else.

"That's it," Grayson says behind me. "I'm done for the day."

I rotate to find him standing up and walking toward me with his wine glass in hand. Instantly, my stomach flutters like a schoolgirl who is about to stand next to her crush. That's what this man does to me and has since that day I ran into him. "Did you notice which wine this is?" he asks, both of us facing each other, our elbows on the railing.

"That cheap but good one that I fell in love with in Sonoma last weekend after I learned there are wines to taste and wines to drink. And that the expensive ones are barely tolerable. Yes. I did. Thank you. I still love it."

"It's a good choice," he says. "And I like that you look beyond the price tag."

Because so many people in his life see his money before they ever, if they ever, see the man. "We should go to that Italian place you love tonight." He leans over and kisses me. "Or we could order in and eat in bed in between fucking and fucking some more."

My cheeks heat and do so despite the fact that I've done about every naughty thing possible with this man. "I do love our nights in bed."

He sets his glass on the ledge next to us and then takes mine and does the same. "Then bed it is." His fingers tangle in my hair, and he drags my mouth to his. "I love you, Mia. You know that, right?"

"I love you, too."

"I mean *I really* love you."

"What's wrong?" I ask, pulling back to look at him, sensing his suddenly darker mood.

"Nothing is wrong. Nothing has been wrong since the day I met you." His mouth closes down on mine, and his tongue strokes deep, his hand settling between my shoulder blades, molding me close. It's a passionate kiss, a hungry kiss. A kiss that is all about emotion and not sex. A kiss that screams "I need you" and says so much more than even words.

It ends with me breathless and his thumb strokes away the dampness on my lips. "I have something for you." He kisses me and then walks to his chair. "Come here."

His mood is hard to read and I tilt my head to study him. "What are you up to, Grayson Bennett?"

"Come find out." His green eyes light with challenge. "If you dare." With those words, the edge I've sensed in him seems to soften.

My lips curve and I join him. "I dared," I say, stepping between him and the chair, my hands settling on his chest. "Now what?"

"Sit and close your eyes."

"Now you're making me curious."

"Good. Sit, baby. You'll like this, I promise."

"Of that, I have no doubt," I assure him because this is him and he gives me no reason to do anything but like and love each day and moment.

I sit.

"Shut your eyes," he orders.

"Eyes shut," I say, doing as commanded.

He kneels beside me or I believe he does. My eyes are, of course, shut. "What if I was to blindfold you?"

My eyes open and meet his sea-green stare. "Is that what you're going to do?"

"Would it be a problem?"

"Of course not. I trust you. Is that what you're going to do?"

"Not until later." He sets an envelope in my lap. "Open it."

My teeth sink into my bottom lip and my curiosity is ripe. I unseal the flap and pull out a contract. "You bought the lighthouse from the man who retired it?"

"I did," he says. "Look at the name on the deed."

I scan and note the extreme price this place cost, and I know he did this for us, for me. "There's no name. I don't understand."

"I want you to fill in your name."

I shove at his chest. "No. No, I won't take this. No." I stand up and he sets the paperwork on the chair and joins me, his hands shackling my waist and pulling me to him. "I want you to have it."

"I want to be here with you. I don't want a present like this. I'm not with you for this."

"What's mine is yours, Mia."

"No. No, that is not true and all I want is you, Grayson. I don't care about the rest."

He cups my face. "I left it blank for a reason. I want your name on that deed, but I want it to be my name."

I blink. "I don't understand."

"Marry me, Mia. I need you forever."

I suck in a breath. "What?"

"I love you. I need you with me forever. Say yes."

"I—I have to sign a prenup. I don't want you to ever think-"

He kisses me, a deep slide of tongue before he says, "Is that a yes?"

"Yes. Yes, you know it is. You know I love you. You know I need you, too. Forever."

His lips, those perfect lips, curve. "Then I have something else for you." He reaches into his pocket and pulls out a satin pouch. "It was easier to carry this in this than in a box today." He removes the stunning, incredible, giant ring inside. "If you don't like it-"

"My God," I say eyeing the emerald-cut diamond that sparkles with hints of blue. "It's gorgeous, but I think I need a security guard to wear it."

He laughs. "I'll be your security guard." He slips it on my finger. "It's a rare blue diamond. I special ordered it. I wanted you to have something no one else would have."

I look at it and then him. "Thank you."

"Thank me by spending the rest of your life with me."

"I wouldn't have it any other way." I swallow hard. "I hate that my mother isn't alive to know you."

"As do I of mine, Mia."

It's one of the things we've bonded on. The love of our parents. The loss of our mothers. Mine to cancer two years ago and his to a car accident five years ago. "Does your father know?"

"Not yet, but he loves you. He'll be happy, but Mia, he'll be harder on you at work. You need to be ready for that."

"I want to prove myself. You know I do. I can handle it."

He cups my face. "It doesn't mean he doesn't love you. Just the opposite. He's hard on me. He always has been."

I can't think about his father right now. I smile. "We're getting married."

He smiles. "Yeah, baby. We're getting married."

CHAPTER ELEVEN

Mía

The present

"We will not part ways in the middle again. I want you. I will fight for you, but we're in or we're out. We're together or we both move on once and for all."

As much as I've told myself that I'm "out" with Grayson, right now—as much as I know I have real reasons for that choice—standing here with him, his body pressed to mine, his words in the air between us, it's not that simple. Especially not here, in the lighthouse where he proposed to me. Right here, right now, the idea of never seeing him again is unbearable.

He cups my face and tilts my face to his. "You aren't going to tell me you're already out?"

"No," I say. "And I should, but no. I'm not."

He strokes my cheek, studying me for a long moment before he says, "Everything I could say to the 'I should' part of that statement, I won't. Right now, I think we both just need to be us again. To just live in the moment."

"I can't do that here. There are too many memories here. Too much to question."

"If you keep saying things like that, I won't hold back what I have to say." He leans in and kisses me. "So yes.

Let's leave. Let's go to the house." He doesn't wait for the confirmation that he knows he'll receive. I'm the one who didn't want to clutter all my good memories of us in this place with the way we are now.

He links the fingers of one of his hands with mine and turns toward the stairwell, leading me that direction, but he doesn't urge me in front of him, as the gentleman that he is might do another time. He goes first. A choice I understand, because I understand him. God, I really do understand this man. Being at my back would have been dominant, and while he's dominant without question, he doesn't want me to feel that he's suffocating me with that dominance. Even so, he doesn't let go of my hand the entire walk down the stairs. He holds onto me and keeps me close and the thing is, I want him to hold onto me. I want him to prove what can't be wrong. That's why I haven't let him try. I know he will fail. I know that once he does, I have to say that final goodbye and I don't know how I survive that. Not now that I'm with him again. That's why I don't want to talk right now. I just need to pretend none of the bad exists. I just need to be with Grayson, and I can't seem to find the will to fight that need.

We step onto the beach, and his arm slides around my shoulders. "What did Eric and Davis say about Ri?"

"Let's not talk about Ri," he says. "That's part of the bad and we don't want that right now, right?"

"Yes. Right."

"What were you thinking about in the lighthouse?"

"Good memories. Not bad. I was standing on the beach, looking at your house, and I just—felt like I was suffocating in everything bad and so I ran there."

"I still went there until after the funeral," he says. "Alone." He looks down at me. "I went there alone, thinking about when I went there with you."

My teeth scrape my bottom lip and I cut my stare. *"Before the funeral,"* I whisper. "You mean before the second time I left?"

"Yes, Mia," he says, "before the second time you left."

We don't look at each other, but that reality hangs in the air between us. That's when he stopped trying to tear down my walls. That's when he let me slam them down between us and keep them down. That's when he moved on. I don't like the idea of him moving on. I've never liked the idea and yet, I have no right to care. I walked away. It doesn't matter that it killed me to do it.

We reach the house and enter through the patio and the minute we're inside the living room, he turns me to him, his fingers lacing into my hair. "After the funeral because you left me not once, but twice. After the funeral, because I needed you so fucking badly and you still left. Again. After the funeral, because that's when I started to question us. That's when I decided that if what we had was real, then you wouldn't have written me off without really hearing me out."

I lower my chin, trying to catch my breath, my hand flattening on his chest. "Words won't fix this."

"Mia—"

I jerk my gaze to his. "And I'm going to tell you what I admitted to myself walking with you from the lighthouse. I didn't want you to try to explain because we both know you can't, and once you can't, we're done. Some illogical part of me, and you know I'm not an illogical person, felt that if you never tried, I could keep clinging to maybe, to that possibility that what we had was real."

"It was real," he says, stepping into me, his hand flattening on my lower back, fingers tightening in my hair. "It *is* real." His mouth comes down on my mouth, and when his tongue strokes mine, I don't even consider holding back. I have craved this man forever it seems. I have needed him eternally. I sink into him and the kiss, I drink in the taste of him, the feel of him, the absolute perfection of him.

His hand slides up my back, settling between my shoulder blades, molding me to him. "I can't stop needing you, Mia. I shouldn't have tried." His mouth is back on mine before I can even fully process those words, his tongue licking into my mouth, stroking and tasting me the way I do him. And he tastes of those words, of need and hunger, of regret and passion. Suddenly I can't get close enough to him, I can't get enough of him.

My hands slide under his T-shirt, a raw need clawing at me. I need and need and need some more. I shove at his shirt and he pulls it over his head, but my hands never leave his perfect body, which he spends hours in the gym making that perfect. I kiss his chest and he drags my sweater over my head, his hands settling on my face, even before it hits the ground. His lips are on mine. We're wild and hungry, and he scoops me up and starts walking. That's when reality hits me.

"Stop!"

He halts, his lashes lowering, and I can see him reaching for restraint. "What are we doing, Mia?" he asks softly.

"Not the bedroom." He stands there a few beats and then starts walking again. "Grayson."

He doesn't reply. He doesn't stop again until he's laying me down on the bed we once shared, and he's on top of me. "This is our bed. That lighthouse is our lighthouse. We're these things, and we need *us* right now. So yes, Mia. In the bed, *our* bed, where I plan to fuck you and make love to you as many times as humanly possible this very weekend and the rest of our lives if I have my way. If you have a problem with that, I need to know now."

CHAPTER TWELVE

Mia

My reasons for not wanting to be in this bed fade with his declaration that it's ours, and that he wants me in it for the rest of our lives. "The only problem I have right this minute is that you aren't kissing me."

He leans in, his lips a breath from mine, but he doesn't kiss me. "Why didn't you want to be here with me?"

"Ask me later. Kiss me now."

"No. You think I've had someone else here, in our bed." It's not a question.

"I don't have the right to ask."

"Is that why you didn't want to be here?"

"Yes," I whisper, my hand settling on his cheek. "But I know—"

"I never brought a woman here or to my place in the city. Just you, Mia. But I can't tell you that I didn't try to fuck you out of my system. I needed to fuck the images of you with Ri out of my head."

"I wasn't with Ri."

"I know that now, but I didn't then. It doesn't matter who it was. The idea of you with someone else drove me crazy. It still does."

"I wasn't with anyone else," I dare to confess, when a part of me doesn't believe he deserves that confession and another feels I owe it to him.

He pulls back to study me. "What?"

"Never. I didn't. Not once. And I told myself that it was because I was busy, trying to build my career, but—"

"But what, Mia?"

"I just wasn't ever ready to let go. I didn't *want* to leave you. But I had to."

"No, baby. You didn't, but I get that you really felt that you did. It hurts, but I get it." His mouth comes down on mine, and I feel as if he's breathing me in. I know I am with him. No. I'm drinking him in, arching into the sweet weight of him on top of me. We kiss with desperation, like two people who need each other to survive, and right now, I don't know how I have survived without him. He rolls us to our sides facing each other, his fingers catching the hook of my bra and just that fast, he's pulling it away, and his hand replaces the silk. His mouth is back on mine and sensations consume me, so many sensations colliding with emotion and need.

"Are you still on the pill?" he asks.

"Yes. I just—I am."

"Good. For now." He kisses me, a quick brush of lips over lips. "I need you naked. I need to feel you next to me." He rolls me to my back and with that "for now" in the air, he moves and resettles with his lips to my stomach and this is not an accidental connection. My heart squeezes with the certainty that he's reminding me of how many times he told me he wanted a little girl just like me. It affects me. We had so many plans. We were best friends. We were so many things that happened so very quickly and easily, and then it was gone.

He pulls down my pants, and all too quickly my sneakers and everything else are gone. I'm naked and not just my body. I am so very naked with this man and always have been. But as for my body, I'm not alone for long. He strips away his clothes, and I lift to my elbows to admire all that sinewy, perfect muscle before he reaches down, grabs my legs and pulls me to him. The minute my backside is on the edge of the bed, he goes down on a knee. I sit up and cup his face. "Not now. Now I need—I need—"

He cups my head and pulls my mouth to his, kissing me with a long stroke of his tongue before he says, "And I need to taste you."

"Not now. I'm not leaving. We have time. I need—you. Here with me."

His eyes soften but he still leans in and licks my clit, and then suckles. I'm all but undone by the sensation because one thing I know and know well is how good this man is with his tongue. But he doesn't ignore my request. He pushes off the floor, and in a heartbeat, he's kissing me and I don't even know how we end up in the center of the bed, our naked bodies entwined. We just are and it's wonderful and right in ways nothing has been in so very long.

He lifts my leg to his thigh and presses his thick erection inside me, filling me in ways that go beyond our bodies; driving deep, his hand on my backside, pulling me into him, pushing into me, but then we don't move. Then we just lay there, intimately connected, lost in the moment and each other. "Is this what you wanted?"

"Yes," I say. "This is what I wanted."

"I didn't think I'd ever have you here, like this, with me again."

"Me either," I whisper, my fingers curling on his jaw. "Grayson," I say for no reason other than I need his name on my lips. I need everything with this man.

He kisses me, a fast, deep, passionate kiss. "I missed the hell out of you, Mia. So *fucking* much. I don't think you really understand how much."

This moment, right here, right now, is one of our raw, honest, perfect moments that has always made his betrayal hard to accept. I need that honesty in my life and with him and I don't even think about denying him my truth. "I missed you, too. More than you know, Grayson."

He squeezes my backside and drives into me again. I pant with the sensations that rip through my body, my hand going to his shoulder. "Nothing was right without you," he says. "Nothing, Mia." He kisses me, and I sink into the connection, pressing into him, into his thrust, into the hard warmth of his entire body. Needing to be close. Needing the things that separated us not to exist.

Our lips part and his mouth is on my breast, lips suckling my nipple, my sex clenching around his shaft with the sensation, a soft whimper escaping my lips. And then he's kissing my neck and whispering in my ear, "I love you, Mia."

And I say it. I have to say it. "I love you, too."

He pulls back to look at me. "Say it again."

"I love you."

He cups my face and forces my gaze to his. "Don't forget that. I'm not going to this time." He doesn't give me time to respond. His mouth crashes down on mine and in a fury of heat, we snap and tumble into that wild, animalistic place that allows nothing but give and take. We're all over each other. We're saying, grinding, pumping, touching, kissing. I don't want it to end and yet I need that next place we're trying to find, I need all that I can take and give with this man, and there is no holding back. I am there, on the edge, and tumbling right over, far too quickly. I stiffen and then my body quakes, arching into Grayson's, my fingers digging into his back. A low guttural sound escapes his lips as he buries his face in my neck and shudders into release right along with me. Because that's just one of the things about us I remember. We're really good at doing things together.

We collapse into the mattress, into each other and for a long time we just hold each other. I'm not sure how long we stay like this. I just know that it can't be long enough. Finally, though, Grayson rolls me to my back and grabs tissues that he offers me, but when he pulls out, he doesn't move. He stays right there with me, his elbows planted on either side of me.

"We need to have a serious conversation, Mia," he says softly.

"I know. I know we do."

"Good. So which will it be? Pizza or Chinese?"

Tension uncoils in my belly and becomes laughter. "Pizza. I haven't had this pizza in—"

"Too long," he says softly, brushing his thumb down my cheek. "Too long, Mia." He kisses me. "I'll order." He lifts away from me and I am instantly cold where I was hot moments before. He sits down beside me and grabs his phone from the nightstand.

I listen as he orders our usual, remembering my preferences like I'd never left him. When he's done, he sits his phone on the nightstand and leans over me. "I'll be right back." He kisses me and then in all his beautiful nakedness, he stands up and walks to the bathroom.

I sit up and take in the room that I haven't really looked at in years, finding it as remarkable and unchanged as the chemistry between me and Grayson. It's a traditional room, the bed an oversized king in black, with thick posts on each corner, and furnishings to match. A sitting room to the left with black leather furnishings and—

Grayson's phone buzzes with a text and my stomach clenches. I throw away the blanket and sit up, staring at it on the nightstand. This is where it ended last time. In this bed, in this room, with a text message I'd accidentally read, but I don't want it to end again, not this time.

I don't want it to end.

I don't want to say goodbye to Grayson.

CHAPTER THIRTEEN

Mia

The past, six months ago

Grayson and I don't speak on the drive from the cemetery to the Long Island mansion that is our destination. When we arrive, he doesn't reach for the panel to key in the code. His hands grip the steering wheel, and I know why. While his father was rarely here in the Hamptons, this was his house. Now it's Grayson's, and I feel the punch in my heart with this knowledge.

"Fuck," he whispers, and when I reach for him, he pulls me to him and kisses me, like I'm breathing life into him, like I'm why he can move forward.

He releases me and rolls down the window, keying in the code. The gate opens and he maneuvers us past it and down the half-moon-shaped drive. We park in the garage, and when he kills the engine, we just sit there in the tiny space, neither of us wanting to move. "He was never here and yet somehow walking into this house, without him being here, makes this all so damn real."

"Because it's a piece of him. It's a part of your life you shared with him. What are you doing about his apartment in the city?"

"I made arrangements. I have a service packing up everything and putting it in storage. I can't go through it now. I need time and I need to sell the place." He laughs bitterly. "He'd be furious if I left it sitting there, creating a useless tax bill."

"He really would," I say, giving him a sad smile. "I can help you go through everything."

He looks over at me. "I need you to help me, Mia."

"Then I will."

He lowers his chin to his chest and draws a deep breath before he opens the door and gets out. By the time I'm out of the car, his fingers are tunneling into my hair and he's pulling me against him. Somehow the door gets shut and I'm against it. And right there, in the garage, next to his father's Mercedes, we're all over each other. It's like an explosion of everything all at once; anger, passion, love, pain, heartache of so many varieties.

My skirt is at my waist, his hand on my bare backside, fingers under the strip of satin running down the center. My hands are under his jacket, at his waistband. He shrugs out of the confines of his jacket and then it happens. We fuck. His pants are shoved down and my panties never come off, but they too, are just shoved away. My leg is at his hip and he presses inside me and I gasp, even as he shackles my backside and lifts me off the ground. My back is against the Porsche, and in a crazy, frenzied rush we pump, grind, and just plain fuck. Only fucking isn't even the right word. We need. We take. He needs more than I do and I just need to help him sate the pain.

When it's over, he all but collapses on top of me, but still, he's so damn strong that he holds me up. He carries me just like that, into the house, and to a small bathroom off the garage entrance, and once I'm on the sink and we're put back together, he cups my face. "Let's go to the lighthouse," he whispers.

I look down at my high heels. "I need to get rid of these."

"Your things are still in the closet."

My lashes lower, a punch of emotion in my chest. My things. He kept my things. He strokes my cheek. "Where they belong, Mia." He doesn't give me time to argue, taking my hand and guiding me through the house, but I wouldn't argue anyway. With this man is where I've belonged since the moment I met him. Every moment apart has felt wrong, and I refused to let myself think about why I left. I won't. Not now. I wish never.

We enter his bedroom, our bedroom until I left because we were here every weekend, and he doesn't stop until we're standing in an enormous, fancy, dressing room closet. He stands me in front of my row of clothes, him at my back, his hands on my shoulders. I stare at my things, at the way they hang next to his, and emotions assail me.

Grayson releases me and we dress, our eyes holding almost the entire time, neither of us looking at our naked bodies. Once we're both in sweats and sneakers, as well as hoodies, we head to the beach. Hand and hand, we walk to the lighthouse and side by side, in a lounge chair we share, we watch the sun set over the ocean. When finally we speak, it's of his father. We talk about him, just him.

Grayson and I spend two days holed up in the mansion. We don't leave. We don't talk about us. Not the broken part of us. We do a lot of remembering the good parts of us. We make love. God, how we make love. We speak in those unspoken ways and I don't ever want to leave him again. But Saturday night arrives, and with it, the reality of a return to the city and my job with Ri's company with it. Grayson and I are in the bed, both in sweats and tees, and I'm lying on his chest while we watch Tombstone, one of his dad's favorite movies, when he suddenly hits mute and rolls us to lay face to face.

"We're out of time. I don't want this hanging over us tomorrow. I have to go back to the city tomorrow night."

"Me, too."

"We go back together."

"Yes," I say. I don't even hesitate. "Together." He strokes hair from my face and I can sense he needs to say more, but I suspect he just doesn't have that in him right now. "Are you hungry?"

"Yes. You?"

"Yes. Pizza or Chinese?"

"Pizza. You know I love the pizza we get here."

"Yes, Mia. I do know you love it."

He says it like it's so much more than pizza. And it is. The way he knows me is everything. He reaches across from me and grabs his phone. He orders the pizza, drops the phone on the bed, and then stands up and heads to the bathroom. His phone buzzes with one of the million text messages he's gotten this weekend and I look down, and I don't mean to, but I read the message.

I pant out a breath and sit up, holding my stomach, tears welling in my eyes. My God. I'm such a fool. I have to leave. I scoot off the bed and Grayson's phone starts ringing. I grab my sneakers off the floor and call out, "Your cell is ringing," before I disappear into the hallway. I collapse against the wall and swipe at my tears. I hate him. I love him so damn much. I have to get out of here. I dart for the living room, grab my purse and exit beachside, where I start running what will be miles of beach to reach a spot where I can catch an Uber. It's time to leave Grayson and our lighthouse behind.

LISA RENEE JONES

CHAPTER FOURTEEN

Mia

The present

"Hey, baby, did my phone buzz?"

I glance up to find Grayson standing in the bathroom doorway, now wearing sweats, his perfect chest naked, and shaving cream all over his face. "Yes," I say. "It vibrated on the nightstand. Why are you shaving?"

"Your face is all red."

I reach up and touch my cheek where the sting of his whiskers remains for the first time in far too long while he rakes his gaze over my naked body. "And if you don't get dressed, you're about to have shaving cream all over you." He winks. "Check the message for me, will you?" He disappears into the bathroom. "Read it out to me!" he calls out.

I inhale and let my breath out, ticking through all the reasons why I am not going to leave.

He left his phone behind last time and now. He didn't feel like he had anything to hide then or now. He's shaving for me. He was always thinking of me. When I went to him at the funeral, we felt real and honest, like we do now. When I'm with him, despite every piece of evidence that says he's guilty, my heart says that he's innocent. If it didn't, I wouldn't be here now trying to protect him; trying to protect someone who I know to be a good, fair, honest person.

I grab his phone and I don't look for anything to cover up with, because naked says I'm willing to be vulnerable with him again. And I have to be if I'm going to stay here, and I am. Everything inside me says that I belong here. I walk into the bathroom and slide between him and the counter.

"I told you to get dressed," he reminds me. "You never did follow orders well."

"That hasn't changed and it won't." I lift his phone and read the message. "It's from Eric." I say, glancing at Grayson and then back to the screen, to add, "he says: *We aren't going to get anyone closer than Mia is to Ri to take him down. You need to be reasonable on this. We'll protect her. You have my word.*" I look up at him. "He's right. I came here to protect you. Let me protect you."

He studies me for two hard seconds and then he grabs a towel, wipes his yet to be shaved face, and tosses it. "No. Not just no. *Hell no*, Mia. I am not making you a target." He walks to the door, grabs my pink silk robe I left here a year ago and pulls it around me.

"No," he says, tying the belt for me. "This isn't a discussion."

"I was always a target, Grayson," I say, sliding my arms into the robe. "Always. He wanted to hurt you. He used me and I let him. *I hate* that I let him. I don't know how to undo that but to go after him for you."

"You're not going to go after anyone. That's what I do. Not you, Mia. *Not* you."

I reject that idea immediately. "You don't go after people. That's one of the things that makes you you and not him. That's one of the reasons why I love you."

"And yet you've spent the last year with him."

"Working at his company, not with him. I didn't lie. I haven't been with anyone, I haven't been with him."

He grabs his phone and exits the bathroom. I feel the blow of his words and it hits me then that if I'm wrong, if he didn't do what he appeared guilty of doing, I'm the bitch. I'm the one that doesn't deserve him. I owe him in so many ways and I decide right then that I love him enough to accept the guilt, because he doesn't feel guilty to me.

I race after him and I exit the bedroom, a gust of wind blasting through the now open patio door. I exit into a chilly breeze to find Grayson standing at the railing facing the ocean, his upper body naked, the muscles in his back and shoulders bunched. I don't even hesitate. I go to him and the minute I'm by his side, he pulls me between him and the railing but he doesn't speak. He just looks at me.

I reach up and brush my hand over his unshaven face, the rasp of whiskers on his jawline, then along the thicker edge of his goatee. "I like having your whisker marks on my face and everywhere else. I miss seeing those marks on my body."

He pulls away the silk tie at my waist, parting my robe and then molding my naked body to his body. "I stood out here wondering if you'd just leave again, Mia. I didn't know for sure that you'd follow me out here. I can't walk out of a room and have you disappear again. If that's where this is headed, then we need to ignore the pizza, fuck again right now, and make it a final goodbye."

"Can we fuck again right here and now before the pizza gets here, and just not say goodbye?"

The buzzer that signals a front gate visitor goes off and Grayson ignores it. "I don't want the fucking pizza. I want us to make a decision about us, *but* we have a pizza at the damn gate." He releases me, grabs his phone and hits a button that opens the gate on his security system app.

I yank my robe shut and his eyes meet mine, heat and anger in the depth of his stare. And then he just turns and leaves the room. It's then that I feel as if I've been punched. It's then that I realize that in the midst of finding each other again, we're closer now to losing each other for good than ever before.

I enter the bedroom and stare at the massive space, and the bed where I have slept so many times with this man wrapped around me. I miss sleeping like that, with him. I don't know how long I stand there imagining those moments with him holding me, but he doesn't come back. Time ticks by and Grayson still doesn't come back to the bedroom.

It's been too long and I hurry down the hallway and start hunting for him. I enter the living room and find the pizza box on the island in the kitchen, but he isn't there. My gaze lifts to the patio, and I know then that he's back outside, but he's chosen to exit through a location that divides us this time. I don't let that dissuade me. I cross the room and exit to find him, just as he was on the other patio, his back to me, leaning on the railing.

"I don't want this to be goodbye, Grayson. I don't know how to make sure it's not goodbye. There's so much bad now. I'm afraid there's too much bad. Are we just here to find that out?"

He inhales and pushes off the railing, turning to look at me, his hands on his hips. "I am angry, Mia. Because being with you, feeling how good it is, makes me wonder if you ever felt what I feel."

"It wouldn't feel this good if I didn't. You know I did."

"Then how can you believe that Ri could set me up with the DA and not set me up that night?" He doesn't give me time to answer. "Eric called. He has a source he's been working for a while now. He's been nickel and diming us with information about Ri, who we knew was up to something. Eric offered him an excessively large sum of cash and he delivered in a big way and fast."

"What does that mean?"

"He says that this plan to take me down has been two years in the making, before my father died, and right after we got together. The reason I believe him is that he named names, people working inside my operation and working for Ri. Two of those people were identified as problems and are already gone."

My stomach knots. "*She* was one of them, right?"

"Yes, Mia. She was one of them."

It's then that I know that Grayson didn't betray me, but instead, I've betrayed him and us.

CHAPTER FIFTEEN

Grayson

The past, a year ago

"She won't answer her phone," I say, standing at the window of Eric's office, the sun dipping beneath the skyline.

He steps to my side. "You yanked her off her case, Grayson," he says. "You didn't warn her. You didn't even talk to her first."

"I'm quite aware of what I did, and you know why. The lead counsel on the case was fired because the feds are breathing down our throats over this case and apparently for good reason."

"I get it. We had a lead counsel playing dirty with a dirty client. You didn't want Mia anywhere near that shit, but you should have warned her."

"If I'd have warned her, she'd have looked at me with those beautiful blue eyes and told me why she should stay on the case."

"Because she's got a perfect, clean record that represents us well. There's logic there." I open my mouth to lay into him and he holds up his hands. "But it's a danger to Mia. I get it. She'd still be dealing with a mobster,

87

defending a mobster. She'd still end up with that reputation of aligning herself with that man."

"Not to mention my father and his damn rule. You lose your first lead case, you're out. And we're going to lose this case."

"The future mother of his grandchildren? Surely not."

"You've known my father since we were both at Harvard. You know his mentality, so yes, even Mia, who he loves, hell, more so *because* he loves her. He calls it tough love. And let's face it. If she was made an exception, that would ruin her here at the firm. She'd be my woman and nothing more, and that's not what she is or what she wants. It's not what *I* want for her."

"You gave the case to Becky. She hates Becky. They're rivals."

"I handed that decision to Mitch. He's the lead partner over the associates. I didn't take that decision from him, nor did I make it for him, but yes, I approved his choice. Becky is cutthroat and disposable. Mia is not."

"A choice that's not in your favor with Mia."

He's right. I don't want him to be, but he is. I scrub my jaw, glancing at my watch, and tick off the four hours since Mia left the office furious. It's seven now and so far the doorman hasn't seen her at the apartment, which means she has to be at her best friend Courtney's house or her father's place. "I need to find her, but I have a conference call with the Lugo Corporation in fifteen minutes."

"I can handle Lugo," Eric says. "I got it. You go."

And because this is Eric, who I trust like a brother, I take his offer. I head for the door and waste no time making my way to my private office. Once I'm inside, I step behind my desk with the intent of gathering my work to take home with me when Becky steps into my office. "I need to talk to you about the case you put me on." She shuts the door and flattens herself against it, her blouse cut low, her red hair free of the clip she normally wears it in and I don't like it any more than I do her style of sexual manipulation. "I heard you're the reason I got the lead on the Pitts case."

"Don't come into my office and shut the door without my permission. Open it."

"I need to talk about this case in private."

"I'm not your supervisor. Mitch Rivers is. Talk to him about who, where, why, and what case. I have someplace to be."

"This case is tricky." She races forward and stops in front of my desk. "The client involved is a mobster."

I do not have time for this woman right now. "If you're over your head Becky, talk to Mitch."

"I'm not over my head and I appreciate you believing in me. I can handle this case. I'm not backing out."

The phone on my desk rings. "Open the fucking door," I say, and hoping the call is from Mia and that she's back in her office, I grab the line without even looking at the extension. "Davis says he needs to see you before you leave," Eric says. "It's urgent."

I give Becky my back. "Define urgent."

"He says the feds want documents you aren't going to want to give them."

My jaw sets hard. "What documents?"

"Do you really want to talk about this on the phone?" Eric asks.

"I'll be right there." I hang up and when I set the receiver back on the desk, I realize that my door is still shut but Becky is no longer in front of my desk.

I rotate to my right to find her on my side of the desk, naked from the waist up. "What the fuck are you doing?"

"Thanking you for the case." She steps into me and I grab her arms, holding her back. "Get dressed. Now." I set her back from me.

My door opens and Mia gasps. "Oh my God," she whispers, and my heart is thundering in my ears, adrenaline surging through me. "It's not what it looks like, Mia. I swear." I release Becky and the stupid bitch wraps her arms around me and presses her breasts to my chest. "Fuck. Get off me." I shove her back and rotate toward the door, but Mia is already turning away. "Mia! Fuck. Mia." Becky comes back at me, wrapping her arms around my waist. "Get the fuck off of me, Becky." I untangle her from my body and I'm around the desk in a blink, chasing after Mia, and I don't give a fuck who knows.

"Mia!" I shout watching her round a corner and damn it, I pray the elevator is shut and slow to reach her.

I race in her direction, but I'm too late. She's in the elevator and I reach the doors right before they close; just in time to see the stricken look on her face, in time to look into her eyes and see the pain, but unable to get to her. "It's not what it looks like!" I call out as the doors shut and immediately head for the stairs. I'm in the stairwell in another blink and I start the run down thirty flights. I exit to the lobby and search for Mia, but she's not there. I charge for the front door and burst onto the street and again, she's not fucking there. I head back inside and scan my surroundings before going back outside. Nothing. I grab my phone from my pocket and I dial Mia.

"Answer, baby. Answer the damn call." But she doesn't answer. I dial again. I send her a text: *It's not what it looked like. I turned my back and she undressed. I swear to God, Mia. It was not what it looked like. She flung herself at me. I love you. You're everything to me.*

I pace the lobby and call the security for our building. "If Mia gets there, I don't care what it takes, you call me, and you keep her there. There's a thousand dollars in it for you. No, five. Five thousand dollars." I hang up and anger takes over the panic.

I walk to the elevator and punch the button, dialing Eric while I wait. "Meet me in Becky's office with the security guard in three minutes." I don't give him time to respond. I hang up and step into the car.

Once I'm inside, I inhale and force out a breath, forcing myself to calm. The floors tick by and I exit, entering the office lobby, but I don't stop. I cut left and walk past the bullpen of cubicles to an office on the right where Eric and the guard are waiting. "Is she in there?" I ask.

"She is," Eric says.

I start forward, step inside and Eric and the guard flank me, then step to my side. Becky is behind her desk, her hair now neatly pulled back at her nape, a look of shock crosses her face, rocketing her to her feet. "What is this?" she demands.

"Pack up and leave," I say. "You're fired."

She blanches. "What? No. You can't fire me." Her voice lifts and takes on a desperate quality. "I'll claim sexual harassment."

I lean on the desk, my fists on the wooden surface. "If you just made me lose Mia, I'll destroy you and enjoy it. Hell, I'll destroy you and enjoy it just for making her feel what she's feeling right now. So you want to sue me? Bring it the fuck on, but get out."

CHAPTER SIXTEEN

Mia

The past, a year ago

I don't know how I make it out of the office building without crying. I don't even know how I get blocks away on foot. I search the area around me and I don't even know where I am. A cab with a light on drives by and I chase after him. He stops. For once a New York City cab driver actually stops for me. I climb inside. "Just drive," I say. "Just drive and there's a big tip in it for you. And ignore me back here." The minute the car starts moving, the inevitable happens. I burst into tears, a fierce, body-quaking explosion. I cry and cry and I don't even try to hold back.

"Big tip," I call out when the driver looks back at me. "Just drive." My phone starts ringing again and I know it's Grayson. Of course it's Grayson. He's busted. He's so very busted. I don't look at my phone. I want to throw it out of the window. I have nowhere to go. I can't go home. It's his home that was clearly never mine. That's what I get for moving in with a man at three months and then accepting a proposal at nine months. "Out—out of the city," I sob to the driver. "A hotel. Queens or Brooklyn. I don't care which. Just take me. A hundred dollars on top of your fare."

I sink back against the cushion and look at my gorgeous special ring that seemed to have so much thought behind it. It meant something. Now it doesn't. It doesn't mean anything. I squeeze my eyes shut and the image of Becky pressed to Grayson, no, her *breasts* pressed against Grayson, twists me in knots. He fired me from the case and gave it to her. Now I know why. My phone rings again and I grab it, stare at Grayson's number and turn it off. It's off. *We're* off. We're over forever.

I start to cry all over again and curl up against the door behind the driver's seat. I lose time inside the tears until finally, the driver stops. "Holiday Inn, sweetheart," the driver says. "That's as good as it gets right now. I'm done driving."

I open my purse, glance at the meter and toss him cash; I always have cash because Grayson always worries I might need it. Or he did. Those days are over. Maybe he didn't worry at all. I exit the car and try to pull myself together. I have to walk into this hotel and get a room without blubbering. I shut the cab door and it races away. I glance around and the airplane overhead tells me I'm close to the airport. Maybe I'll just fly away and go somewhere. It's not like I have a job now. Grayson owns that, too. I think I let him own everything I am and that was okay when I thought I had everything he was, but I was wrong. I didn't have all of him. I had nothing and I have nothing.

I swipe at my cheeks and walk into the hotel lobby. I actually hold it together. I'm proud of myself. I grab my key and once I make it into the room, I'm done holding it together. I melt down right there at the door. I sink to the floor. I lie there. Time passes and passes and I just don't stop hurting. I don't even know when I come to enough to realize that I'm in the dark. I don't care, though. I dig in my purse and turn my phone back on. Grayson calls immediately and I hit "decline" and dial my friend, Courtney, because now I have to admit my hell to someone, and who better than my best friend since childhood?

"Mia!" she says. "Grayson is looking for you. He's worried sick. What's happening?"

"I need you to come to me. I need you."

"Are you okay?"

"I'm not dying or anything, even if I feel like it. Just come."

"Where are you?" she asks, urgently.

"I don't know. Hold on." I push to my feet and flip on a light.

"You don't know?!" she asks incredulously. "Were you kidnapped? Do we need the police? Are you okay?"

"If only those things were true." I sit down on the king-sized bed with a stupid orange comforter, when orange happens to be Grayson's favorite color. Or not. I don't know what is real anymore. "I'm in a Holiday Inn in Queens. I just told the cab driver to take me wherever." I give her the address.

"I got it. Mia, *what* is going on?"

"Just come here and do not, and I mean *do not*, tell Grayson where I am or you aren't a friend." I hang up and walk to the window, pulling open the basic cream-colored curtains to spy the "liquor" sign. I'm not a drinker, but I need to be sedated right now.

I glance down and realize I've smartly settled my purse over my chest and it rests at my hip. Smartly, because I'm really barely hanging on right now. I find the key to the room on the floor by the door and grab it, sticking it in my purse. A short walk down the hallway and I'm exiting onto a street in what looks like a crappy neighborhood, but hey,

I grew up in a crappy neighborhood. I'm just fine in this one. I cross the street, enter the store and walk to the counter. "Where's the cheapest bubbly you have?"

The lady behind the counter, who has dark hair speckled with gray and seems to be missing a front tooth, looks me up and down. "You don't look like you need cheap. That's an expensive purse at your hip which means your outfit is expensive, too."

"Yeah, well, I'd tell you I had a rich guy that fucked around on me and now I'm alone, but I bought these clothes and the purse on my own. And you bet your ass they're expensive. I worked for them, not him, because I don't need his damn money. It was never about his money."

"Wow, honey. Fridge. Far right. Buy two. Spumante. It tastes good when everything else tastes bad."

"How much?"

"Ten dollars a bottle."

I yank a hundred out of my purse and stick it on the counter. "Keep the change. He's buying the booze."

She hands me a paper bag and two plastic cups. "One for now and one for later," she says.

A few minutes later, I enter my room, struggle to get the stupid bottle to pop and then sit down on the loveseat against the wall where I guzzle the bubbly right from the bottle. My phone starts ringing, on the nightstand where I apparently left it, and I take my bottle with me to check it just in case it's Courtney. It's not. It's Eric.

I answer. "What do you want, Eric?"

"He didn't do it, Mia. He's devastated. He's freaking out. It was a set-up. He was—"

"Stop. Just stop. You're his best friend. You're like brothers. You'd say anything to protect him."

"I would, but I'm not. He didn't do this. He *loves* you. He needs you."

"I'm not coming back. I'll send the ring. I'll send my credit cards he gave me. I don't want his money. I don't want him or that job either."

"Mia, be reasonable."

"Reasonable?! Did you really just say that to me? Go away and take him with you."

"Mia. *Mia.*" Suddenly, I'm not talking to Eric anymore and it's not him saying my name.

At the sound of Grayson's voice, I can't breathe. I hurt so badly. So very badly. "Go away," I whisper, but I'm not even sure he can hear me. I hang up and throw my phone. I start to cry again and I don't stop until my phone rings like ten times in a row.

"Courtney," I whisper and I force myself to get up, kicking off my heels to pad across the carpet. My phone confirms Courtney has called four times. I call her back.

"Which room?" she asks.

I open my door and look at the number. "331."

"I'm on my way up."

I flip the lock to prop the door open and walk to the sofa, where I sit down. I've downed another drink and I'm starting to feel the blessed buzz when Courtney appears in the doorway, her blonde hair in disarray, her red dress ripped. "What happened?"

"Don't ask." She shuts the door and drops her purse on the floor. "He called me. He says—"

"I walked in on him with Becky's naked breasts pressed against him."

"He says she—"

"Don't. Don't you too. I saw it. Do you not understand that I saw it?" My phone rings in my hand and I toss it. "Just help me plan the rest of my life without him."

97

"Right now. We're going to order pizza, you need food because that bottle is half empty and you don't drink. As in, you get drunk at half a glass."

Her phone rings in her hand and she glances down at it. She answers the line. "Yes. She's—"

"Are you talking to him?" I demand.

She stands up and holds up her hand. "Mia."

"You are. I can't believe you took his call. Hang up."

"Hold on," she says into her phone and punches a button. "She's on speaker."

"Mia, I didn't do this," Grayson says. "I swear on my mother, my father, and to God."

"Stop talking, Grayson, because you see, I'm stupid. I listen to you. I want to believe you. Or I did. I trusted you. I would have died for you. No more. *No more!*"

"Baby, I'll do anything—"

"To get your baby-making machine back? So you can look perfect and have your heir? No. I'm not her. I'm taking off the ring and Courtney will bring it to you. Maybe you can put it on her. She can be—"

"Stop, Mia," Courtney says. "Stop."

"He fired me off my case and put her on it, Courtney!" I shout. "Did he tell you that?"

She pales. "What?"

"Yes. Fired me and then fucked her. Or fucked me and fucked her. I don't know. Hang up."

"Mia!" Grayson calls out. "Listen to me. I—"

My stomach rolls and I rush to the bathroom and end up on my knees at the toilet. I heave and I am so sick I want to die. When I finally fall back on the tile, Courtney kneels beside me. "Honey, I hung up. I didn't know about the case. That's—"

"Damning?"

"Yeah. It kind of is."

I curl up in a ball and let the ring in my hand settle on the tile. "Take it to him and try to get my things. I need to be alone."

"I'll deal with all of that tomorrow. I'm staying with you tonight, but let's go to my place."

"He'll find me there."

"Well, we have a friend who's a realtor. I'll see if she can get you into a place tomorrow, but you need to be somewhere where you can deal with paperwork. Let's go back to the city."

I sit up and pull my knees to my chest. "Right. Because I need a home and a new job."

Because I don't live or work with Grayson anymore.

CHAPTER SEVENTEEN

Mia

The present

I'm still standing on the patio of Grayson's Hamptons home, in nothing but a silk robe I bought when he was mine and I was his. I'm staring at him and he's staring at me, and there are steps and space between us that reach beyond the physical. The night we broke up is right here with us, a wedge that won't collapse. Images of Becky pressed against him pound at my mind, driven home by that damn text message I'd read the night of his father's funeral. It zaps that blame I'd put on myself. It says that I'm not the one who betrayed us. It says *he* did. It's the message that could catch him in a lie. I don't want him to lie, but I need to know if he will. Emotions rush at me hard and fast. I need the truth once and for all, but I can't do this in this robe. I can't be that vulnerable.

I rotate and exit the patio, hurrying through the living room and I don't stop until I'm in the bedroom. I hunt down my clothes and sneakers, scoop them up and retreat to the closet. I've just managed to fully dress when Grayson appears in the doorway, and he too now wears a T-shirt with his sweats and sneakers. "Leaving again, Mia?"

"Not yet, but you're right. If I leave this time, it will be for good. Tell me," I order, my voice cracking. "When did you start fucking her?"

He curses and runs his hand through his hair, his dark waves left in disarray as his hands settle on his waist. "Really, Mia? That's where we're still at right now?"

"Tell me," I order again. "Just say it all. *Say it all.*"

He is in front of me in a snap, pulling me to him, his body absorbing mine and not gently. "There is no *when*, Mia. I was not, and *have not* been with Becky. She came into my office. She shut the door. I told her to leave. The phone rang. I thought it was you. I was hoping it was you since you'd shut me out over pulling you off the case. I turned my back and took the call. It was Eric with a problem. When I turned around, she'd stripped and rounded my desk. She flung herself at me and then you opened the door. I don't know how the hell it was planned that well, but it was planned."

"Mitch," I say, my throat going dry, my hand flattening on his chest, heat rushing up my arm. "He called me and told me that there was a blowup on the case and that it was critical I get to your office right then."

"And you took Mitch's call, but not mine?"

"I was furious with you, Grayson." I twist out of his arms and move to the opposite side of the dresser that sits in the middle of the closet. "You pulled me off the case and didn't talk to me about it in advance. *Me.* The woman lying naked next to you in bed every night"—I hold up a hand—"but that's another subject. Mitch still works for you. Mitch clearly made sure I saw you and Becky together, which means he's working against you."

"Becky and I were not together, Mia. Holy hell, woman. What do I have to do to get you to understand that?"

"You can't," I say, emotions welling in my throat. "You can't."

"Then why are we even here right now?"

"Right. Why? I'll leave." I round the dresser, but he catches my arm and pulls me to him.

"Are you really going to do this to us over a lie?"

"Ask why I left after the funeral?"

"I take it that's a yes. A lie that isn't mine destroys us."

"I read your text message that day. You went to the bathroom and it was under my arm on the bed and I read it: *Grayson, I saw Mia with you. I didn't want to come up to you and start a war. Thinking of you. Love, Becky.*"

He blanches and I've never seen Grayson blanch. "First, Becky never had my number. I have no clue how she would get it. I have no relationship with her. And the day of the funeral, the whole weekend of the funeral, I had hundreds of messages and barely glanced at any of them. I was focused on my father and you." He releases me and reaches for his phone, snagging it from his pocket. "She signed it Becky?"

"Yes," I whisper, hugging myself.

He types in the name in the search bar and pulls up the message. "And there it is," he says, his lips thinning. "That little bitch. I didn't read it or respond to it." He hands me his phone. "I didn't respond to most of the messages I got that day. You know how this goes. People use everything, including death, as an excuse to try to get a piece of me. I didn't have it in me to deal with any of that. I didn't respond to anything for days after you left and I didn't try to catch up. You can see her message and all the rest that are unread and without response."

I blanch, shocked by the idea of such a complete shutdown. "None of them?"

"I wouldn't even talk to Eric for a week after my father died and you left. Leslie had to come knocking on the door because I didn't respond to her either. And when I did come out of the haze, anyone that mattered had already found another way to talk to me. The last thing I wanted to do was read the damn messages. Go through my phone, Mia. There is no interaction between me and another woman. Nothing. Because there is no other woman."

I start to shake and I drop his phone without meaning to, but neither of us reach for it. "You really didn't do it?"

"No, baby. How could I want anyone but you? We were, we *are*, in love and it's a passionate love." He pulls me to him. "The kind of love most people never find." He strokes hair from my face. "Tell me you believe me."

Air lodges in my throat and I press a hand over my mouth, holding back a sob. I hurt him. I hurt him in a way that's unforgivable. "I left you the night of the funeral. I'm such a horrible bitch."

"No," he says, pulling my hand from my face, his fingers tangling in my hair, tilting my gaze to his. "There were devious people at play here. People who meant to break us up to hurt me. And I promise you, Mia, they will pay for the pain they caused you, caused *us*."

"I left you after your father died. You can't forgive me for that. How can you even consider trying?"

"We were fighting when this happened. And it was a big fight. You already felt betrayed. I'm not blind to my part of this. I made mistakes that made this possible."

"Yes. I was angry. And yes, there are reasons we were fighting. The case you pulled me off of. The timing. It was everything at once. It was—it was more than Becky and things we need to talk about, but those things weren't me leaving you after your father died. I betrayed us."

"No, baby. You didn't. I did. I let us be that vulnerable. I did things that day that I didn't explain. I allowed us to be that exposed and it won't ever happen again. I'll protect us. I'll protect you. And Ri will pay in blood for what he's done."

Anger quakes in his voice and Grayson is not a man who allows such emotions to control him. Anger that I know is not all about Ri and what he perceives his role to be in our breakup. It's about me leaving him, me walking away. No matter what he says otherwise, we've betrayed each other in ways that have led us to where we are now. We can't just kiss and make up. We have to fight through the emotional storm to follow. We have to fight for each other.

"We're going to be okay," he promises, and I wonder if he's trying to convince me or him, or both of us. It doesn't matter though. I want him to be right. I want him to be right so badly that when his mouth comes down on mine, I am instantly clinging to him the way I would a ledge for dear life. I can't let go or I'll cease to exist. I won't let go. Not this time. Not ever. No matter how fierce that storm becomes. No matter how brutal the fight I know is to come.

CHAPTER EIGHTEEN

Mia

"Stop kissing me like it's goodbye, Mia," Grayson orders, pressing me against the closet wall in between a row of his clothes and mine. His fingers tangle roughly in my hair. "There is no goodbye. Not this time. Not ever again. You're mine and just to be clear, I'm yours. I was *always* yours."

"We can't pretend it didn't happen. Things happened. Those things change us."

He kisses me, a deep, drugging kiss. "Do we taste different to you?" His hand slides down my back and he cups my backside, molding my hips to his hips, his erection pressed to my belly. "Do we feel different? How do we feel, Mia?"

"Perfect," I whisper. "But we aren't perfect. We can't pretend that we are." Emotions overwhelm me, the idea that I left him after his father died cutting me into a million little pieces. "Grayson—"

"We're back together. That's what matters. We can talk, fight, fuck, and repeat to get past this, but we have that opportunity for one reason and one reason only. We're here. We're together."

"We're together," I whisper, my hands sliding under his shirt, palms pressing against his taut flesh in an effort to confirm those words that don't yet feel real.

"I don't want to be without you again," he says, his voice low, raspy, affected, as his mouth closes down on mine and the minute our tongues connect, we're desperate all over again. Our hands are everywhere and clothes are shoved, pulled, and pushed until we're standing there in the closet, naked, and it's still not enough.

Grayson pulls my leg to his hip and his thick erection presses along the wet seam of my sex. I moan with need and satisfaction because he's here, we're here, doing this. He presses inside me and lifts me at the same time. It's just like beside the car the day of the funeral. He's holding me and his hands squeeze my ass, pulling me away from the wall and down on top of him even as he's pushing into me. I hold onto his shoulders, my nails digging in, my lips finding his as his hand settles between my shoulder blades. And when we can't kiss for the force of our passion, I bury my face in his neck, inhaling that delicious woodsy scent of him that I want to roll around in, get drunk on.

It's as if we both feel like we have to hold onto each other, to get closer to survive and perhaps that's where this leads; we do have to hold onto each other, we do have to get closer to survive all the damaged places we've been and now we cannot fully escape. I don't want this to end, and yet when my back hits the wall again and he drives into me, I welcome the tumble into bliss that follows. I welcome the shudder of his body around mine. I revel in the deep, guttural groan that escapes his lips in pleasure with me and no one else. Our bodies tremble and ease, seconds ticking before Grayson eases back and says, "How about that pizza?"

I laugh, "Yes. Please. I'm officially starving."

He kisses me, a quick brush of our mouths before he settles me on the ground, but when we would pull on our clothes, he cups my face and tilts my gaze to his. "We're together, Mia. Everything will work out."

"I want it, too. I really did hurt without you, Grayson."

"Me too, baby. Me, too." He strokes my hair. "Let's eat in the kitchen where we can heat up the pizza and talk. *Really* talk. I owe you a few more explanations."

He means about why he fired me off my case the day we broke up and I dread this conversation. I'm not even sure I can have it now. I don't want to fight with him and yet I know we need to clear the air. I know I've avoided conversations that I shouldn't have avoided. I think he feels the same thing, the dread, the wish that we could just go back to where we started. I sense it in the air, I see it in his eyes. He doesn't want to fight, but we have to have tough conversations. We have to deal with this.

As soon as we're both back in our sweats, tees, and sneakers, Grayson takes my hand and leads me forward, out of the bedroom. Once we're on the stairs, he bends our elbows, pulling me next to him. "Talk, fight, fuck," he says softly, and the new ball of dread in my belly softens when we enter the kitchen and seem to fall into old habits. He kisses my hand before he releases me to place the pizza in the oven. "Do you remember the first time we ate this pizza?" he asks, turning up the temperature.

Do I remember?

So very well.

"How can I forget our first date?" I ask, settling onto a barstool. "It was a week after our meeting for drinks, and I still hadn't called you on Friday night, so you took matters into your own hands."

"I had no choice," he says, joining me to sit on the barstool next to me, both of us facing each other, his hand settling on my knee. "I wasn't letting you run from me."

"I wasn't running."

"You were, Mia. You were running scared. I saw it in your eyes."

I cut my stare and think back to that night, to where I was in my head when I met Grayson because it feels a lot like where I am with him now. And I know Grayson. I know that's the point in this conversation. He knows that, and he wants me to tap into that memory, into those feelings, and the way he freed me from them. No. The way *we* freed me from them.

Grayson cups my head, and kisses me. "How about some wine, baby?"

"Yes. Please. Do you have that one—"

"Of course I have that one. It's what you like." He stands up and crosses the room to another bar at the end of the kitchen while I let my mind go where he wants it to go. To our first real date:

It's seven on Friday night and the cubicles beyond my office door are all empty. I gather my work and slide it into my briefcase. My cellphone rings and I grab it to find my father calling. "Hey, dad."

"You still at work?"

"I am. You?"

"Not tonight. I'm headed to a baseball game with my new foreman, Cameron, and then we're going to the casino in Connecticut."

"The casino? You don't like to gamble."

"That's what they make penny slots for," he says. "And I need a break. I'm burning it at both ends. What about you? The new job burning you out?"

"No," I say. "I love it. It's—interesting." As is the boss, who I keep thinking about way too much, but thankfully haven't seen again since our bar meet-up.

"We need to meet up for dinner. I know the job is new, but come to Brooklyn, honey. I need to hug my daughter. How about next weekend?"

"I'd like that. We'll make it work."

We chat a minute more, then disconnect and I'm bothered by the call. My father gambling? That makes no sense, but that home builders show he went to a few months back did earn him lots of new woodworking business. Maybe his money situation has eased up. I need to talk to him next weekend, but it must have if he's taking time off.

Relieved by this idea, I grab my briefcase and head for my door. I'm about to exit when Grayson steps in front of me and I do what I did once before. I smash right into him. I gasp and he catches my waist. "I do like the way you keep running into me," he says, those green eyes piercing mine. "You haven't called."

I should step back. I should push away from him. "No, and I won't." I inhale and try to step back.

He holds onto me. "Do you want me to let you go?"

"That's a trick question," I answer honestly.

"Explain, Mia."

"If you weren't my boss—"

"I'm not your boss, Mia. I'm just a man who can't stop thinking about you. Have dinner with me."

"I can't."

"You want to."

"Yes," I agree.

"Then you can," he counters.

"I can't get by the fact that you're Grayson Bennett."

"To most people, that's not a problem."

"I'm not most people," I say. "I told you that."

He stares at me several beats and then his hand falls away. "I'll see you soon, Mia." He backs out of the office and disappears.

I sink against my wall just inside the doorway and try to catch my breath, but my God, my entire body is on fire. He's just so damn—perfect. The way he looks. The way he smells. The way he feels. Those green eyes. I breathe out and force myself to move.

I exit my office and scan for Grayson but he's nowhere around, and a punch of disappointment grinds through me. He's my boss, no matter how he tries to frame it otherwise. I can't go out with him. I can't even sleep with him. It sucks. I hurry forward and enter the elevator, my body humming a tune that Grayson wrote. I need a workout. A long, hard workout. And chocolate. It's not Grayson Bennett, but it will do. My weekend plans set, I exit the building and start walking. I've made it one block, with one to go to reach the subway, when a black Porsche pulls up next to me.

The window rolls down. "Get in," a male voice calls out and I suck in air when I realize it's Grayson. It's a moment of decision. I know this. I should say no. I try.

I walk to the window and lean in. "I'm not getting in."

"No one else knows what happens between us unless we make that decision together. It's just you and me tonight, Mia."

Just me and him. I don't know why those words, all of them spoken together, hit all the right notes, but they do. "I don't want to regret this," I say, in a last bid for resistance.

"And if you walk away, will you regret that? Because I can tell you, I will."

I tell myself he's a man that already controls my job. I can't allow him to become the man who controls my heart and yet, I don't know what happens. I just—I get in the car.

Grayson sits back down next to me and hands me my glass of wine. "What are you thinking, Mia?"

"About you showing up in your fancy sports car and telling me to get in." I reach up and stroke his cheek, the rasp of his whiskers on my fingers. "And then you brought me here, to your mansion in the Hamptons, in a chopper. But we had pizza as your way to prove to me that you were just a man. That we weren't worlds apart."

"We were never worlds apart," he says. "From the day we met, we were a team."

"And yet you fired me off that case without talking to me first," I say, the words spilling out of my mouth of their own accord. "I don't understand how that made us a team. It made you the man in control of my heart and my career."

"And so instead of fighting with me, instead of giving me a chance to explain, repent, regret, make it up to you, you used Becky as an excuse to run."

"I didn't run." I try to stand up.

He catches my arm. "What are you doing right now?"

CHAPTER NINETEEN

Mia

"What am I doing right now?" I demand, still on the barstool with Grayson holding onto my arm. "Giving myself room to fight. I don't want to be trapped in my seat right now."

He studies me for several unreadable seconds and then lets me go, but there's something in the way he does it, in the way he withdraws beyond the physical that keeps me in my seat. "I'm not even thinking about leaving. I wish I never had. I wish I could turn back the clock and get back our lost time."

He doesn't immediately respond. He doesn't agree. He doesn't offer me the forgiveness I don't deserve for leaving, and some part of me really needs to be forgiven, perhaps because I feel he never really will. Which makes the fact that he's the one who stands up now and walks away, appropriate. He offers me his back and presses his hands onto the counter opposite the island by the sink. I've hurt him again, and in turn, I've pushed him away when I want him close. I stand up and quickly slide between him and the sink, but he doesn't move. He doesn't touch me. "Is that how it is, Mia?" he asks. "I suffocate you? I make you feel trapped?"

My hand settles on his chest. "No. God no. You always made me feel safe in too many ways to name. In *us*. In the rest of the world. In my desire to go bigger and further. You made me feel so many things, good things that I have missed. I just—"

"You just what?" he demands, his voice low, taut, and still he doesn't touch me.

"I felt like that safe feeling was a lie. I was so hurt when I left that I think it's hard to let down my guard again."

"I didn't cheat on you, Mia. I don't deserve to have you put up that kind of guard again."

"I know, but I pulled up a guard to protect myself and now I have to pull that wall down. I *am* pulling it down. The problem is that when I pull it down, what's left is me leaving you over a lie that wasn't yours. That makes us unsteady."

"To me, unsteady was when we were apart. Steady is here, now. Together."

"It is, but you own your world in a way that most do not. You own my world and *me* when I'm with you. With my heart on the line, that's more than scary. It's terrifying."

"And you own mine, Mia. You *are* my world."

He says the words with deep, guttural passion, but he still doesn't touch me. "I think it's hard to feel like your equal," I admit, just wanting to say it, to get it all out once and for all.

"When have I ever made you feel less than me?" He pushes off the counter, his hands settling at his hips, withdrawing even further. "I talked to you about everything. I trusted you with everything. I needed you with me through it all."

"But you have to know that there are few human beings on this planet that can stand next to you and not compare themselves and judge themselves unworthy. I always wanted to deserve to be by your side. I wanted to have more depth to what I offer when you do ask my opinion."

"And you thought you didn't? Aside from being beautiful and intelligent, Mia, you, like my father, have a moral compass that keeps mine in line. He loved that about you just like I do. You keep me solid."

"You don't need me for that. Your father carved right and wrong into your very being. I want to be more than that for you and for me. That was something I was working toward when we broke up and it felt good. I need my own successes, so when you pulled me from that case without talking to me, I felt—owned, in the wrong way."

"Mia—"

I hold up a hand. "Before you respond, I need to say a little more. You handled pulling me from that account wrong, but I had insecurities that probably made me handle it just as wrong. Had Becky not pressed her damn naked breasts against you that day, I would have talked it out with you. That's what I'm doing now. I'm talking it out with you. Not running."

"I was protecting you," he says. "That is what the man who loves you should do."

"If I was at risk of your father firing me to set an example, I should be making the decision about taking that risk."

"It was more than that. I get that you were next in line, but we pulled the lead counsel because he was in bed with the mob. That's how we ended up defending a dirty mobster we thought wasn't dirty. You didn't see all of the facts and when I did, I pulled a favor with the judge. I asked to have the opportunity to pull you. He made me do it on the spot. It was then or never and I didn't want you on the feds' or the mob's radar. The end. That wasn't happening. I love you too damn much for that."

"You should have told me you were making the call. I don't know a woman who would be upset that her man was trying to protect her. I just don't get why you didn't talk to me. That isn't us. Not the us I knew."

"I had to make a snap decision and I know you, Mia. You would've said you could take the heat off with the feds."

"I could have. I'm squeaky clean. I would have if it protected you and the firm."

"That's what I mean. You would have tried to protect me. I would have pulled you, and the fact that I ignored your pleas would have made it worse."

"No. It would not have because I wouldn't have felt betrayed. Just pissed." I step to him again and press my hand to his chest. "Don't do that to me again because we will need a weekend and a rubber room for the war that will ensue."

"If I ever have to make a snap decision to protect you, Mia, I'll make it and I'd expect you to do the same in reverse." He shackles my arm and pulls me to him. "Like you came here to protect me. That's what we do. We protect each other. That's what you would have tried to do."

I reach up and brush my fingers over his jaw. "Yes. We protect each other, but next time, you don't get to go around me."

"You're right, but just know this, baby. When I look into your eyes and you ask for something, it's hard as hell to deny you." The buzzer on the oven goes off.

"Even pizza? Because I'm really hungry."

He cups my face, and he's not focused on pizza. "If you hold back, if you get ready for me to leave you, then you've already left me again. Or just never came back. All in, Mia, or all out."

"All in," I say, despite the fact that I am unreasonably afraid of being hurt. He didn't betray me. I betrayed him. I hurt him. I need to be vulnerable. I owe him that. And I have to trust him not to hurt me, the way I should have trusted him a year ago.

"How about that pizza?" Grayson asks, kissing me. "It's been far too long since we shared one together."

"Pizza with you sounds like everything."

Tension eases from his body, and the hard lines of his handsome face soften. He's back. He's here with me and relief washes over me. I need him. I need him in ways I tried to deny and failed every time.

He walks to the oven and pulls out the pizza and I turn to watch him return. He sets it on the island counter. "How's your dad?" he asks, flipping open the lid.

My eyes go wide. "Going out of town this weekend and I don't have my phone. What if he calls?" I dart away toward the bedroom and hunt down my purse and my phone. Once I've located it, I check my missed calls and go cold. Ri has called not once but three times.

I glance at my text messages and there's one there from him as well: *Mia. We should talk. Immediately. Call me.*

CHAPTER TWENTY

Mia

I've barely read the message from Ri when Grayson appears in the closet doorway. "Is everything okay?"

I don't even consider anything but honesty with Grayson, not now, not ever before. "I have missed calls from Ri." I offer him my phone. "And a text message."

He steps forward and takes it, glancing at the message. "Fuck Ri. Let's go eat our pizza." He grabs me and starts to walk with my phone still in his hand.

I catch his arm and dig my heels in. "Wait."

"You are not working for him if that's what you're about to say," he says, rotating to face me. "You don't need him, his job, or his money. You have me."

"I know that, but until we hear more from your team about whatever he's up to, I think we need to hear what he has to say. Just let me do some information-grabbing."

"I've had about all of you with Ri that I care to handle, Mia."

His voice vibrates with anger, the kind of anger I deserve considering I left him over a lie that wasn't his. The kind of anger that tells me he's affected by my leaving, *we're* affected, no matter how much we both just want to go back to the old, untainted us.

"I can't take back what I did," I say, "but I can make it work for you and us. I'm protecting you, and as you said, that's what we do. We protect each other. It's a call. That's all, and you already know he's up to trouble. Let me find out what I can with you right here with me."

His lashes lower, his expression all hard lines and angles, seconds ticking by before he looks at me and says, "Make the call. Get it over with." He looks down at my phone and I swear there is this moment when he realizes he's holding it captive as if he didn't even know he'd done it. And that's not Grayson.

I push to my toes and kiss him and it feels really good to have him right here where I can do that. "Getting it over with now," I say, settling on my feet and taking my phone from him. Grayson leans on the dresser in the center of the closet, his back pressed to the wooden surface. I do the same next to him, making sure my legs are aligned with his, making sure he knows that I'm right here with him.

Only then do I hit the callback button for Ri. He answers on the first ring.

"Mia," he says.

"Ri."

"I called you an hour ago."

"I didn't hear it ring," I reply, glancing at Grayson with a question in my eyes. Can he hear?

He gives a nod.

"Word is that you're looking for a job," Ri snaps.

I don't play coy, which is another form of a lie and I hate lies. "You've been an ass to me since that incident, Ri. I haven't been feeling exactly secure."

"It's against your employment contract to hunt for a job without offering notice first," he replies, no denial of the incident or his treatment of me since. "That bonus I gave you when you signed on. I could strip it."

122

I glance at Grayson who smirks, because obviously money isn't exactly a good threat to use against me right about now. I assume I'll move in with him again. I assume I'll have a job with him should I so choose. I assume we'll get married, but—what if those things don't apply? Grayson must see the questions in my eyes because he steps in front of me, his legs caging me. His eyes hold mine and there is pure possessive heat in his stare, and with it, a promise that I am his and he is mine.

"Mia?" Ri snaps.

I force myself to focus on the call and Ri's threat, which may or may not mean he knows I'm back with Grayson. Ri is sneaky. He'd test me. He'd trick me. "I'm just trying to digest what you just said to me. Come on, Ri. You know how awkward it's been and that's personal, not professional. Only it's become professional because I now fear for my job."

He inhales sharply. "I gave you a job. I gave you a sign-on bonus. I waited for you to get over him. Why the fuck can't you just forget him like he has you? He's all over the papers with that model."

That cuts and I look down, afraid I won't control my reaction to Ri as well if I look into Grayson's eyes right now. I left him. He thought I was with Ri. He hasn't lied to me about being with other women. "I have won every case I've taken since joining the firm, two of which went to trial, the rest I settled otherwise. I've done a good job for you and if that's not enough, I need to find another job, and you need to consider this my official notice, which I'll follow up in writing."

He's silent a beat. "We should meet. Now. Tonight."

"I'm not meeting you, Ri. Not unless it's at the office Monday morning."

"Jesus, woman. You're still so fucking hung up on Grayson that you can't see how good I could be for you. He's gone. Leave him in the grave where he belongs."

In the grave. I don't like those words and my gaze jerks to Grayson's, anger burning in the depth of his stare. "Did you hire me for my skills or because I was Grayson's scorned woman?"

"I wouldn't have hired you if you didn't have skills, and it's not my fault that Grayson was stupid enough to fuck around and lose you, personally and professionally. We need to meet."

"Monday morning," I say. "If that's not good enough, fire me."

"You have another job offer," he assumes. "That's why you're pushing back."

"I don't have another job, but I can't take the way you're treating me. It's been an eyeopener. I finally woke up and saw the writing on the wall. I'm not a token in a game you and Grayson are playing. I want to do my job and do it well."

He's silent several beats. "Monday morning. Seven a.m. in my office." He hangs up.

Grayson takes the phone from me and sets it on the dresser behind me. His hands shackle my waist. "I have never wanted to cause someone harm until Ri. He's using that model, who I didn't fuck, by the way, to push your buttons. To push mine."

"I know," I whisper.

"But it still upset you."

"The idea of you with someone else—yeah. That's what even got me to the point of that date with Ri that resulted in a knee."

"Just like Becky sent you to his doorstep," he says as if that's a fact before he pushes off the dresser, withdrawing.

"No," I say quickly. "That's not what happened. That's not even close to what happened."

His jaw clenches. "Do you intend to meet with him Monday morning?"

"I think, under the circumstances, with him going after you, that's a decision we should make together."

"You going anywhere near Ri again is not a smart decision for us, Mia." He turns and walks out of the closet, leaving me trying to catch my breath.

There it is and it didn't take long. Already, we're there, peeling back the layers that reveal his resentment over my stupid actions and he's justified. I quickly follow him, ready to fight for the man I love. I find him in the bedroom, sitting in an oversized black leather chair in the corner of the room, a chair where we have fucked many times. A chair where I've fallen asleep in his arms while we talked afterward. I cross and sink down next to him, but he doesn't turn to look at me.

"I need to know how you ended up with him, Mia." He looks at me, those green eyes turbulent, and yet unreadable. "I didn't think I needed to know, but I do."

CHAPTER TWENTY-ONE

Mia

I don't deny Grayson his request. If he wants to know how I ended up working for Ri, I'll tell him. I want him to know. I *need* him to know. I move out of the chair we're sharing and sit on the ottoman in front of him. And I go back in time, taking him there with me...

Two weeks and seven pounds lost since Grayson and I split, I stand at the window of my new apartment, watching rain pound the Manhattan streets. I should be relieved to have this place, considering it came fully furnished, with a one-year lease, and a fabulous price, but it's just so damn empty, like I am right now. I miss Grayson so much and every time he calls I just want to talk to him, but I miss him too much to do that right now. I'll believe anything he says. I need to believe he's innocent, but every time I travel down that rabbit hole, I wake up from a nightmare involving him and Becky's stupid naked breasts.

My cellphone rings and I walk to the basic wooden kitchen table in the corner of the loft-style space and grab my phone to find my father calling. "Honey, you haven't been out to see me in weeks."

"I know. Sorry. It's been crazy."

"You and your billionaire fiancé are up to fun things, I hope. Are you two in the city by chance? I had to come in for business."

"I'm here. Where are you?"

He gives me a location which isn't far from here. I suggest the coffee shop on the corner because I figure inviting him here would shock him. I have to tell him about Grayson. We hang up and my cellphone rings with Grayson's number. God. I want to take the call. I want to just hear his voice. I hit the answer button. "Mia, baby. Please. Mia, I need to see you. This is killing me."

I start to cry. Damn it, I can't cry before I see my father. "I shouldn't have answered." *I hang up. I want to call back. He calls back. I hit decline and set my phone down, rubbing my palms down my jeans.* Don't pick it back up. Don't talk to him. *His voice, that rough masculine timbre, God, I love his voice so much. It's just perfect, the way I thought he was.*

I grab my black Chanel trench coat, which I bought myself with my first bonus check from the Bennett firm, earned fair and square with hard work. Once I've pulled it on, I settle my purse strap on my shoulder and pick up my phone as it rings again. I'm about to turn it off when a text buzzes and I dare to read it: Mia, I love you. I can't even breathe without you. Come home.

Home? *I type in my first text response to him through all of this.* I never had a home with you. I just thought I did. And that hurts. You hurt me. You can't fix it.

I turn off my phone and stare down at my naked ring finger. I inhale and stick my phone in my pocket. I hurry out of my new apartment, that will never be home but at least it's mine, and rush down the narrow stairs leading to the street. It's not a fancy building, but it's in a safe area. I've barely settled at my table when my father walks in. I wave at him and he heads in my direction, and in jeans and a T-shirt that hug a fit body, his brown hair still thick at fifty-five, he's still a catch, but today he looks weary... definitely weary.

I stand when he approaches and he gives me a hug. "I need some caffeine. Give me a quick minute."

I nod and he walks to the counter, scrubbing his jaw as he does. Weary. Stressed. Worried. Those words go through my head over and over until he's sitting in front of me. "What going on with my daughter?"

"What's wrong?"

He narrows his eyes on me. "You always could read me, heck you read everyone. That's why you're a damn good attorney."

"Yes. What's wrong?"

"I took a loan to grow the business that I'm struggling to pay back. I went to the bank to try to get a loan to pay back the loan. As crazy as that sounds. No go on that. It sucks. The business is growing, but these homebuilders pay at ninety days. I just don't have the cash flow to float the money, which is a common problem for companies growing."

"I'll help. How much are the payments?"

"No. I'm not having that rich fiancé of yours thinking your father is taking advantage. That's not happening."

"Dad, I'll help. Not Grayson." I have it on the tip of my tongue to tell him about the breakup, but something holds me back. "How much?"

His phone buzzes with a text. He grabs it and looks at it. "That's the bank. They want to see me again. You won't need to help. This has to be good news." He squeezes my hand. "Sorry to run off."

"Can you call me afterward?"

"Yes, but don't worry. All is well. This is good news."

He doesn't believe it's good news. I see it in his face. I watch him leave and there is a knot that expands in my belly. I press my hands to my face. I wasted a week crying and I just started sending out resumes. I need a job. "Mia."

I look up to find Ri, or rather Riley Montgomery, standing above me. He's rich. He's powerful. He went to school with Grayson and hates him, yet they cross paths too often and Grayson believes this is no coincidence. "What are you doing here, Ri?"

"I got your address off a resume floating around, but you didn't answer your door. I walked in for coffee and here you are." He motions to the seat. "Can I join you?"

No, I think. "Why?"

He sits down, his dark hair a rumpled mess that somehow still looks planned on him. Everything about this man, including his good looks, feels planned. He's the tall, good-looking, and today he's in expensive jeans and a T-shirt that probably cost a few hundred bucks. That's how he operates. He flaunts his money, while Grayson does not.

"I want to hire you," he says. "I'll up your pay with Bennett by twenty-five percent and give you a fifty-thousand-dollar sign-on bonus."

"Why?"

"You're a star in the making, and if Grayson managed to lose you, I'm happy to sweep in and take advantage. We're growing. We're expanding nationally. We need talent."

"Expanding nationally. Like Bennett. How very Grayson of you."

"I assure you, Mia, that nothing about me resembles Grayson. You have twenty-four hours to decide."

"I'm not fucking you. I'm not doing anything to hurt Grayson."

He laughs. "Do you want that in your employment contract?"

"No. I don't want the job."

He smirks. "Think about it." He slides a card in front of me. "My personal cell is on there. It's a good offer. And if Grayson is really gone from your life, if you've left him behind, why wouldn't you take it?" He stands up and starts walking.

I watch him exit the coffee shop and there is no part of me even slightly tempted to take his offer. I grab my phone, turn it on and text my father: Call me after your meeting.

Feeling the need to do something, to get out of this chair, I leave Ri's card on the table, push to my feet and hurry out of the coffee shop, my path taking me back to my building. I don't let myself read the text messages from Grayson. Once I'm back inside my apartment, I sit down at the kitchen table and start working on resumes again. I have a few interviews. I have money saved because Grayson never let me spend any of my earnings. He was good to me, but now I feel like a kept woman. Isn't that how it works? A rich guy takes care of you and then you look the other way? Except I didn't want his money. I wanted him.

I start working, sending out resume after resume with custom cover letters, and I try repeatedly to reach my father with no luck. It's several hours later when there is a knock on the door. My heart starts to race. Did Grayson find me? I will myself to calm down and walk to the door. "Who is it?"

"Delivery."

"What delivery?"

An envelope slides under my door. I frown and open it to find a picture of a man with a scar down his face with a note on top:

Mia,

I thought you'd want to know the kind of person your father borrowed money from. Don't be too hard on him. This guy is good at convincing people he's legit until they default.

The job offer stands, as does the sign-on bonus.

—Ri

My throat is dry. My heart is still racing. I walk to the table and sit down and start reviewing the information in the envelope and it's terrifying. I press my fist to my forehead and then before I can stop myself, I dial Grayson. "Mia?"

I just sit there, with his voice radiating through me, that voice, that wonderful, perfect voice.

"I love you, Mia. Come home."

Home. *My home with him. "You know that I have to do what I have to do to survive, right?"*

"What does that mean?" he asks.

"It means I still love you, but I have to survive. I have to make decisions—"

"Mia—" I hang up and I grab the card Ri included in the folder and dial.

"Mia," he greets me.

"Email me the offer."

"And that's how I ended up with Ri," I say, finishing my story.

Grayson studies me as he has the entire time I've been talking, more stone than man, his expression unreadable. Abruptly, he stands up and I'm on my feet with him in an instant, not about to let him walk away. "Grayson—"

"Why didn't you come to me?"

"I was going to when I called, but then I had this realization."

"What realization, Mia?"

"That if I took your money, it would seem like I was using you, and too many people use you. We might have been over, but I didn't want us to end with me holding a hand out. That's not who I am and I guess I just needed you to know that I was real."

He pulls me to him. "Damn it, woman. I wouldn't have thought that. You know I care about your father. Some part of you knew, even then, that I'd do anything for you."

"Because you will doesn't mean it's right for me to ask." I swallow hard. "And everyone does. I see how people want a piece of you."

He tangles his fingers into my hair. "And what about you, Mia? What do you want?"

"You. Just you."

"Ask me what I want."

"What do you want Grayson?"

"Everything this time, Mia. I didn't have it last time, or you wouldn't have left as easily as you did." He doesn't give me time to tell him no one could have more of me than he did, than he *does*. His mouth closes down on mine, and that chair, our perfect fucking, talking, *us* chair, is calling us.

CHAPTER TWENTY-TWO

Grayson

I pull Mia down in the chair, resting against the cushion as she settles her head onto my chest. I have not laid with this woman in my arms like this in what feels like an eternity. And so I hold her now, and damn it, I should never have let her go. I should have known that she would never betray me with Ri and her reasons for going to work for him, well, as much as I hate them, they also represent so many of the reasons I love this woman. My money is nothing to her. She's proven that every day of our lives together. She didn't even keep the ring and damn it, that gutted me, and that's exactly where my head goes. The day I'd found out she'd taken a job with Ri and the day the ring found its way back to me...

Three weeks without Mia.

It might as well be the three thousand years it feels like. I can't sleep. I can't think. I can't fucking breathe. I toss my pen down on my desk and stand up, walking to the window, staring out over the city without really seeing it. I just see Mia's pain. "Coffee and a protein bar," Eric says from the doorway.

I turn to find him kicking the door shut and walking my direction in a pale blue pinstriped suit which he only wears on "lucky" days. It's his deal uniform. I'd normally ask what's in the pipeline when I see that suit. Right now, I don't give a shit. "Since when do you bring me coffee?" I ask.

"You need something, man, and I figure caffeine is about as close to good as I can give you right now." He stops beside me and hands me the cup, then reaches into his pocket and hands me the protein bar. "And you need to fucking eat."

I take the damn bar and stuff it in my pocket, but I don't ignore the coffee. I take a sip. "What do you have for me?" I ask, certain him and his blue suit are here on business.

"The bids on the hotel properties were accepted. We officially have locations for the Dallas and New York City Bennett Hotel launches. The firsts of many. Once we ink, I'll work on getting the Dallas law offices moved to the property."

"And we make money on the property where we run our firm," I say. "You're brilliant, Eric. I'm quite certain your bonus will buy you a new lucky suit."

"Try a new lucky Jaguar or ten." He inhales, his mood shifting. "We need to talk."

I narrow my eyes on him. "Talk?"

"About Mia."

Tension radiates up my spine. "What about Mia?"

"She took a job."

My lashes lower and I turn away. She's officially gone. She's not coming back to work here. "Where?"

"That's the part I'd rather leave out of this equation."

I cut him a sharp look. "What does that mean?"

"Ri," he says. "She went to work for Ri."

Those words punch me in the chest so hard that I want to punch the window, and that's not me, that not how I operate. "Is she fucking him?" I ask, the anger I can't control radiating in my voice.

"I don't know, man. I wouldn't have thought she'd take a job with him. Not Ri. She knows how much he hates you."

I love you, she'd said on the phone days ago. More like she fucking hates me. "Leave," I order softly.

"Grayson—"

"Eric, man, I love you, but get out of my fucking office. I need to be alone."

"Right. I understand." He turns and heads for the door. He's just exited when Nancy, my forty-two-year-old, quiet, always smart assistant appears in the doorway, proving she's not smart right now. Otherwise, she wouldn't be about to speak to me. She shoves her black-rimmed glasses up her nose and clears her throat. "Courtney is here. She's a—"

"I know who she is," I snap because of course, I know Mia's best friend. I look skyward and then say, "Send her in."

I stay where I'm at, needing control in a way I normally assume in less obvious ways. Courtney walks into my office and shuts the door. She's wearing funeral black, her blonde hair a mess, which tells me she's a mess, which isn't like her. "I know about Ri," I say.

She reaches into her purse and closes the space between us and I'm aware of her hand in that bag, waiting to deliver another blow. "She gave this to me three weeks ago to give to you and I didn't. I thought she'd take it back, but I can't hold on to a hundred-thousand-dollar ring." She pulls her hand from the bag and hands me Mia's ring box.

"Two hundred thousand," I say, not because the money matters to me, but because of the impact of Mia *giving it back. She never wanted my money. Fuck. She's perfect, and in this moment I know the war is lost. She's gone. I'm not getting her back.*

I take the box.

Courtney opens her mouth and shuts it. And then she turns and walks toward the door. A minute later, she's gone and the door is shut and my mind goes where I don't want it to go. The timing of the news about Mia with Ri and this ring are hard to ignore, no matter what Courtney claims about the timing. Mia's made it clear to me that she's with Ri now and I know she knows that's the end for me, for us.

"Grayson?"

I blink back to the present to find Mia looking up at me. "Yeah, baby?"

Her eyes soften and warm. "God, I missed you calling me that. I just missed you, period. Please tell me what you're thinking."

"You could have sold the ring to help your father."

"Sell my ring? I wouldn't sell my ring. It's—special. It was—"

I tangle my fingers in her hair and pull her mouth to mine. "I know you wouldn't. I doubted you, too, though. You know that, right?"

"You thought I went to Ri to hurt you."

"Yes. I found out you went to work for him the same day Courtney brought me back the ring."

"But I gave her the ring the day we broke up."

"She didn't bring it to me."

"She brought it the day you found out?"

"Yes. She did."

She sits up and climbs on top of me, her hands going to my cheeks. "That must have felt like a 'fuck you' and it wasn't. I would never—"

"I know. I should have known there was more going on than met the eye, but damn it, Mia, you should have known I wouldn't fuck around on you. We were not as strong as I thought."

"Don't say that. Please don't say that. I thought we were perfect."

I turn her over, and lay her on her back, pressing my leg between hers, and I lean over her. "So did I. Maybe that was the problem."

"I don't understand."

"We're human. We're flawed. We can't be perfect. We need to remember that this time. We need to know that it's our flaws, our imperfections, and how they come together to be perfect that makes us perfect. But we have to see the flaws and deal with them to get to perfect."

"And what were our flaws?"

"That's what we need to figure out, baby." I stroke her cheek. "That's what we need to figure out, and if we do, we'll be stronger. We'll be better this go around."

"Promise me because I suddenly feel like the room is spinning like we're uncertain."

"I promise you that there is nothing uncertain about my love for you or my intention to keep you this time."

She strokes my cheek. "I promise you that there is nothing uncertain about my love for you or my intention to keep *you* this time."

I push off the chair and take her with me, carrying her to the bed, where I plan to hold her tonight and every night going forward, but I know that means dealing with our flaws. I know that means admitting we have them.

A long time later, I lay in bed with her in front of me, holding her close, and I think of that ring. I'm going to give it back to her, but not until I know she will never take it off again, and right now, I don't know that and I don't think she does either.

CHAPTER TWENTY-THREE

Mía

I wake to a dark room, the heavy, warm feeling of Grayson holding me, and the spicy wonderful scent of him that I've missed so very much. I smile, snuggling closer to Grayson, and he tightens his grip around me, that safe feeling I told him he makes me feel in full force right now. My lashes flutter and I slip back into that half-slumber state of pure bliss where I get to enjoy who I'm with and where I am without getting out of bed. Only I don't stay awake. I'm just too relaxed and comfortable and I feel the inevitability of sleep as the world goes dark.

The next time I wake I become aware of my surroundings, there's a dull light peeking beneath the curtains and a shift of the bed behind me. "Grayson?"

"You rest, baby," he murmurs next to my ear, his breath a warm trickle on my neck. "I need to go make some phone calls."

"Do you have to go?"

"I'm not going anywhere for long," he promises. "You sleep. I'll be back here with you when you wake up." He kisses my neck and then he's gone.

I stay where I'm at, listening to him dress, and a few seconds later, he appears on this side of the bed in a pair of sweats and disappears into the bathroom. If this was a year ago, I'd go back to sleep. I'd feel safe and secure, and really, I do now—I do, at least, when Grayson's with me, but he's not. He's up. He's moving. He's leaving the room and right now, this morning, I feel like we're dealing with those flaws that he named. Flaws. I really hate that word.

I squeeze my eyes shut and replay last night's conversation with Grayson about that word. When I open my eyes, Grayson is exiting the bathroom, pulling a T-shirt over his head and by the time it's in place, he's left the room. I tell myself to go back to sleep, to just relax into the perfection of being back here with him, but I can't.

Those phone calls he needs to make are likely about Ri and I need to be a part of fixing what problems I helped create. And I did help create them. I was used in a dangerous game Ri was, *is*, playing with Grayson. I sit up and throw away the blanket, leaving myself shivering as a chill touches my naked skin. I quickly walk across the room, enter the bathroom, and a few minutes later, my teeth and hair are brushed, my face washed, and I've pulled on sweats and a tee just in case we have company.

I hurry down the hallway and as I round the corner, the deep rumble of Grayson's voice lifts in the air. I enter the living room and spy him in the connected kitchen standing behind the island with the phone on the counter, obviously on speaker as he says, "I have no idea, Eric." He looks up and his eyes light on me and then warm, his gaze sweeping over me in that familiar, always hungry way that says he wants to gobble me up. I really do love when this man wants to gobble me up.

"How the hell would Becky even get your number?" Eric asks. "You never gave that bitch your number." I am human enough to approve of this reply from Eric and I step between Grayson and the counter, my hands settling on his chest, as Eric continues with, "She left the damn state after you promised to ruin her and before we ever found out what the fuck that set-up was all about."

My eyes go wide, and Grayson shackles my waist, pulling me against him, his fingers tangling into my hair. "Betrayal," Grayson says, his lips near mine. "It was always about betrayal." I'm not sure I like that reply and how it relates to our breakup, but his mouth comes down on mine, his tongue delivering a seductive caress that I feel from head to toe. Fighting a moan, I melt right there in the kitchen, a big puddle of need and want, my hand sliding under Grayson's T-shirt, while Eric is forgotten.

That is until he says, "Grayson? Hello? Are you there?" and I realize that perhaps he's been talking and I didn't notice.

Grayson's lips part from mine, a curve to his mouth as he says, "I'm here."

"And?" Eric prods.

"And what?" Grayson asks, his lips nearing mine again, a warm trickle of his breath promising another kiss I really want and now.

Eric laughs. "Okay. You're distracted. Good morning, Mia."

Grayson and I both laugh. "Morning, Eric," I greet.

"Glad to have you back, sweetheart," he says, "but I need his attention."

I push to my toes and kiss Grayson. "And I need coffee." I dart away from Grayson and call out, "He's all yours, Eric."

"I'm all yours, Eric," Grayson mimics, pressing his hands to the island while I think about those hands on my body. He has *really* good hands.

"I hired a new hacking expert," Eric says. "He's going to dig for answers on this Ri/DA situation and look for ties between Becky and Ri that we might have missed in the past."

"And Mitch," Grayson says, as I stick a pod of coffee in the Keurig. "Mia and I think he helped setup the Becky incident. That could mean that he's on board with Ri."

"Mitch," Eric says. "Interesting. As is the idea that Ri plotted to break up you and Mia to distract you while he landed a larger blow."

That statement guts me. I helped Ri set Grayson up. How do we come back from that?

"I'll have Mitch monitored," Eric adds. "Maybe he *is* the one helping Ri set you up."

"If Ri has the DA interested in taking me down," Grayson says, "it's a lot broader than Mitch, but he might be our door to answers."

That very accurate statement is unsettling in its content, but I'm relieved that Grayson is taking this threat seriously. Ri is coming for Grayson and he's coming in a big way. I know it. I feel it. "Davis just texted me," Eric says. "He wants to meet and talk about this threat from Ri. He says he has pressing information."

"What information?" I ask urgently, forgetting my coffee and joining Grayson back at the island.

"He said it's better talked about in person," Eric explains. "Our chopper is at two, Grayson. How about noon?"

"If your chopper is at two," Grayson says, "Mia and I will fly out on our own a few hours later but, yes, twelve is fine. We'll see you then."

I turn to Grayson. "If he won't talk about it on the phone, it's something bad, right?"

"Something sensitive," he says. "Which doesn't always mean it's bad."

"But this situation—Grayson, if the DA—"

"We'll head off the problem," he says, cupping my face. "Thanks to you, Mia."

"But what if—"

The doorbell rings and we both say, "Leslie," at the same time, referencing his godmother, the woman who was his mother's best friend, and who now protects Grayson like he is her own. We both know this because she's the only person, outside of me, that he allows to enter the gates without his approval first.

"I love her," I whisper, "but I really want to talk about this Ri situation. And I really just want to be with you right now."

"She's going to be ecstatic to see you." He strokes my hair, tender in a way that defies what a hard businessman he is. "Go make her day and answer the door. I'll call Eric back and see if I can get anything else out of him." He kisses me and turns away, already walking toward the patio, which to me is telling. He's concerned and he's trying not to show it.

I force myself to walk toward the front door and I yank it open. Leslie stands there looking as elegant and pretty as ever, her dark hair shiny and perfect. Her petite frame and perfect skin defy her age, which she teasingly changes all the time, but it's older than she looks. Of that, I'm certain. Her expression is that of shock and then pleasure. "Mia!" She rushes forward and hugs me. "You're back," she says, leaning back to look at me. "You are back, right?"

"Yes," I say. "I'm back and this time for good." And I have never meant any words more than I do those.

A few minutes later, Leslie and I are in the kitchen drinking coffee, but Grayson hasn't appeared. I do my best to eagerly interact with Leslie, but I'm worried. Ri is setting Grayson up in a way that would destroy him and maybe even put him behind bars. I can't let that happen, and that means I have to use my leverage with Ri, but Grayson won't like it. He'll forbid it and that's going to be a problem.

CHAPTER TWENTY-FOUR

Mia

I spend a good twenty minutes at the kitchen island chatting with Leslie with no sign of Grayson returning from the patio, which is starting to worry me. "I have cookies in the car I didn't bring in," Leslie says. "I brought them for Grayson to take back to the city."

"Your famous oatmeal raisin?" I ask eagerly.

"Of course, and you know that I love that you love them." She holds up a finger. "I'll be right back." She hurries away and my gaze slides to the patio door where I will Grayson to appear, but still, he doesn't. I finish off my coffee and set the mug in the sink, pressing my hands to the granite counter and praying desperately that I didn't find out about Ri's plan to hurt Grayson too late to stop it from becoming a major problem. I spend about three minutes reminding myself that Grayson is filthy rich, honest, and powerful. He also has thousands of attorneys surrounding him. He'll beat this.

"I'm back with the cookies!" Leslie announces, and I eagerly rotate to face her finding her holding open a Tupperware filled with cookies. "Breakfast of champions," she adds.

"Indeed it is," I say, and I welcome the distraction of a cookie for breakfast. "I really missed these and you," I declare as I finish off the scrumptious treat.

"I missed you, too," she says, her tone sobering. "He missed you, Mia. He wasn't right without you. He just wasn't. He was—"

When I might ask her to expand on that thought, she seems to shake herself, and then refocus. "You have a full Tupperware container of cookies. You and Grayson can take them back to your place and—oh—well, I mean if you're living with him again. Are you back at the apartment?"

I don't know how to reply, and a million emotions assail me. The apartment. *Our* apartment. The place I called home with Grayson. Am I going back there? I want to. I so want to, but—the flaws. The problems. "She shouldn't have ever left," Grayson says, appearing across from me, and then rounding the island to pull me under his arm and next to him. "As far as I'm concerned," he says, looking at me, not Leslie, "with me is where she belongs."

Heat and emotions rush through me. "I'll let you two have some time," Leslie says. "Obviously this reunion is new. Make it a good one, you two." She winks and heads for the door.

Grayson and I stand there, watching her leave and the minute the door shuts, I turn in his arms and stare up at him. "You're right," I say. "I shouldn't have ever left. I regret that more every minute I'm with you again."

"Then you're coming home."

"What about our flaws?" I ask, feeling insecure when I've never felt such things with Grayson.

His hand settles on my cheek. "Baby, we're the most perfect thing in my life, but perhaps that's the flaw. My inability, *our* inabilities, to see a flaw because seeing a flaw means we make sure that we deal with it before we let it hurt us. Come home, baby. Move back into *our home*."

"Yes," I say with no hesitation. "Yes, I want to come home."

He cups my face. "That's what I wanted to hear." He kisses me. "Let's go take a shower."

"Yes, but—"

He scoops me up and starts walking toward the bedroom. "Grayson, what about the call? What did Eric say?"

"Absolutely nothing new."

"You were talking to him forever."

He enters the bedroom and crosses to the bathroom, setting me down in front of the shower. "Grayson, I'm worried. What did he say?"

He drags my tee over my head. "I was sidetracked by a call from Japan." He molds me close, unhooks my bra and kisses me. "Remember? I bought into a convention center in Tokyo."

"Right. I still can't get my head around that. That's a huge buy-in."

"Yes. It was. It kept me busy. I had to stay busy while you were gone."

And he did. He tried to fuck me out of his system. It's not a good thought, but it's also not one I can blame him for. I left. I distrusted him. He pulls his shirt over his head and turns on the shower. "We should go see it soon," he adds, dragging me into the shower.

"I'd like that," I say, as he molds me close, the spray of warm water all but blocked by his big, wonderful body. "Have you ever been to Tokyo?"

"Not with you," he replies, backing me into the corner, his fingers tangling into my hair, the thick ridge of his erection nestled between my legs. "There are so many things I want to do with you and experience with you, Mia. Things I've seen and I want you to see. Things I haven't seen and I want to see with you for the first time." His mouth closes down on mine, tongue flicking against mine, and I moan with the possessive taste of him. There is no part of me that doesn't want this man, and as much as I fear there will be a part of him that doesn't want me that's not what I feel.

He cups my backside and squeezes, his cheek coming to rest against mine, his lips at my ear, "So many things I want to do to you." He presses inside me and his mouth crashes down on mine, and at least for now our flaws disappear. There is no Ri, there is no past, there is only the future, where I want to live forever.

Hours later, Grayson and I have both dressed, him in jeans and a T-shirt, all black, while I choose a soft emerald green blouse and faded jeans. We both pack up for the return to the city and then finally sit at the island and eat the pizza we didn't get to last night, or rather, order a fresh one to enjoy. We talk about Japan, a project he's excited about and I gobble up every detail, the way I always had in the past. He wants to take me there and there is this question in the air that we don't discuss about my future: Will I go back to work for Bennett? It's not a topic we dive into now, not when him pulling me off that case was what really left us vulnerable for a breakup. But that topic is coming and coming soon. I have to go back to work on Monday. I *will* go back to work Monday, and I *will* meet with Ri. No matter how Grayson feels about it. We're going to fight, but this time I'm not leaving when we do. This time I'm going to fight and win because it's about protecting him, something I've failed at miserably.

Grayson feels this topic in the air as well. I see it in his eyes and sense it in his mood, so much so that when Eric and Davis arrive and he stands up to let them in, he stops by my chair, tilts my head back and says, "I won't make the same mistakes again. You have my word." He kisses me and heads toward the door, and I know he's talking about pulling me off that case.

He wants me to come back to work with him, but right now we're about to find out more about the threat against Grayson. We're about to find out how hard we all have to fight. My mind goes back to that interview at the DA's office and the words of one of the men talking about Grayson: *I love taking down a rich fucker who thinks his shit doesn't stink. I'm going to get about ten promotions for burying that rich, fake do-gooder.*

I want Eric and Davis to walk in the door and tell us that this problem is over and that I can just leave Ri behind, but I know deep in my gut they won't.

CHAPTER TWENTY-FIVE

Mia

I'm still behind the island when Eric and Davis, two men I know well, enter the connected living room area. Both good looking, confident, in jeans and T-shirts, which on Davis feels weird, awkward almost, but Eric is another story. Eric is an ex-Navy SEAL with a Harvard background, a brilliant financial mind, and a sleeve of tattoos down one arm. He's someone who manages to feel comfortable in every moment, while Davis prefers the edge of discomfort.

Grayson is on their heels and he immediately crosses to stand beside me, the action an assumption that the other two men will join us on the opposite side. Instead, they halt in the living area, a good distance away from us, too far for a real conversation. "We need to see you alone," Davis announces, speaking to Grayson and obviously shutting me out.

"Mia is with me," Grayson says. "That means she's with us."

"And yet she was with Ri," Davis replies, and like anyone close to Grayson, he actually has the courage to look at me when he makes that statement. "How do we know she's not being inserted now to weaken you?"

"I'm on Team Mia, for the record," Eric quickly adds.

"My job is to protect you, Grayson," Davis argues. "And beyond my job, you're a friend. I don't want you fucked any more than you already are."

"What does that mean?" I ask quickly. "Fucked how?"

"Yes," Grayson says. "What *does* that mean?"

"I really must insist that I speak to you alone," Davis says.

My temper snaps. "I didn't sleep with Ri, Davis," I state. "I was never with Ri. He gave me a job with a sign-on bonus at a time when my father was in debt to a bunch of very bad people. I wasn't going to ask Grayson for money. What kind of bitch would I be to use him for money? I couldn't do that to him or us, and when Ri tried to force a personal relationship, I started looking for a job, which is why I was at the DA's office. And in case you don't remember, Davis, I saw a naked woman pressed against the man I love, *my fiancé*. I wasn't in a good place emotionally, I was dying inside, but I still loved him. I didn't, I wouldn't, I haven't ever tried to hurt him." I press my hands to the counter. "Questions?"

Davis stares at me for several intense moments and then eyes Grayson, who says, "Can we get down to business now?"

Davis shifts his attention back to me. "You always did have a way of getting to the point. Welcome back, Mia."

Eric joins us at the island, pressing his hands on the tile. "Mia," he greets, standing directly across from me.

I slide the cookies toward him. "Leslie made them."

"Oatmeal raisin?" he asks hopefully.

"Yes," I say, looking at Davis. "None for you."

"Fuck, Mia," he says. "Have a heart, will you?"

I laugh. "No. You're a bastard. No cookie for you."

"You know I'm just protecting him," he says.

"Which," I say, "is the only reason I forgive you."

"What did you find out?" Grayson asks. "Is there a collaboration with the DA to take me down?"

"Yes," Davis says. "There is, and it's already six feet deep with layers of evidence."

An explosion of fear for Grayson rocks me, but he's calm, cool, his tone even as he asks, "Evidence of what?"

"Money laundering, racketeering, bribing judges, the list goes on and on," Davis states. "This is an elaborate set-up that might have taken years of work."

"Which brings me to Mia," Eric says.

"Me?" I ask, stiffening while Grayson's hand settles on my back, a silent show of support.

"You," he says. "I think the Becky show was supposed to break you two up. It was supposed to distract Grayson."

I pant out a breath. "I think so, too. I've been thinking that for about twelve hours straight, and believe me, it's a painful realization."

"None of us saw it," Grayson says. "Not me. Not you. Not the people around us."

"That number that texted you the day of the funeral," Eric says, "it was made from a phone that's had two users since and none were Becky. We're working on more."

"Back to the here and now," Davis says, "and my prior suggestion. We need to pick a criminal attorney, a killer that you trust and that isn't connected to the firm."

"He's right," I say, and this time I don't argue for me to handle this. This is too big for my experience and I'm too close to Grayson. "You have no idea who's working for Ri," I add. "You need someone who's a proven winner."

"Agreed," Eric chimes in and looks at Grayson. "Reid Maxwell," he says, glancing at me to explain. "He's one of the attorneys handling the Japan convention center," before he adds, "He has ties to a couple of the best criminal attorneys in the country who happen to own the same firm."

"What ties?" Grayson asks.

"His sister is married to one of them," Eric says. "He represented one of them against the DA over a misconduct case, and the misconduct was against the DA."

"Both are good choices," Davis says, "but Reese Summer is married to Cat of the Cat Does Crime column and when she gets behind him and his cases, she influences a lot of minds. I'd go with Reese. He's the best of the best and she's a bonus."

"Get me a number," Grayson says. "Where are we on finding the mole?"

"I brought in a new security team. One of my old SEAL buddies works with them. I trust him. We won't deal with Ri's influence. They're doing a sweep of our operations to find our moles nationwide. They assure me they'll have an initial evaluation here locally done in two days. They're good. We'll get results."

"How long do we have before charges are filed?" I ask.

"Uncertain," Davis said. "But my source feels it's weeks out, but not months. Weeks. That's not long."

"What else?" Grayson asks.

Davis looks at me. "The closer she is to you, the more chance Ri gets nervous and tries to speed things up." He shifts his attention to Grayson. "She needs to stay away and if you love her, you'll listen. I'm protecting you and her. Ri could smear her just to burn you deeper."

Grayson doesn't reject his words and I suddenly want to explode in protest, but not now with Eric and Davis here. Grayson looks at Eric. "What are your thoughts?"

"I'm not sure Mia being with you matters," he says. "It's all about positioning. If she stays, how do you make that work for you?"

Grayson stiffens, and I know he doesn't like that answer. "Where are we on leverage against Ri?"

"The security team I hired has a master hacker on their payroll," Eric says. "More soon."

Grayson nods. "I'll see you both in the city," he says.

Both men look like they want to argue, but they don't. They turn and leave. The minute the door shuts, Grayson pulls me to him. "I need you to go to Japan, work on that convention center project, and get out of target range until I make this go away."

And so, the war begins. The war between me and Grayson, not Grayson and Ri, because he knows what I know. I'm not a master hacker, but I'm inside Ri's operation, I'm close to him. He needs me here. "No," I say, preparing for the storm to follow as I add, "I'm not leaving."

CHAPTER TWENTY-SIX

Mia

The past, two and a half years ago

"I should not be in this car with you," I say, glancing over at Grayson as he navigates his Porsche through Manhattan traffic, the man and the car radiating sexiness and power.

"We're just going for pizza," he says, turning a corner.

"In the Hamptons," I say. "I can't go to the Hamptons with you."

"Why not?" he asks.

"All the reasons I didn't call you. All the reasons I already told you I can't see you."

"And yet you got in the car," he points out.

"I know." I swallow hard. "Grayson."

"Yes, Mia?"

"Can you stop the car?"

"At the chopper pick-up, yes."

"I'm the kind of girl who's fine with a slice of pizza at the corner pizza joint. Can we just do that before you leave?"

"We're already here." He pulls us into a parking lot for the chopper service that I knew was nearby but never gave much thought to it until now.

"And there's a pizza spot one block down. I'll even buy."
I give a strained laugh. "I just got this great new job, you
know?"

He kills the engine and turns to face me. "I'll bring you
back tonight if you want to come back. No one is going to
know we did this but you and me, Mia. I'll protect your
privacy. I'll protect *you*."

"Not by helping me at work," I say quickly, rotating to
face him as he does the same of me. "That's not what you
mean, right?" I press. "I'm not doing this for special
treatment. I don't need that. I don't want that. That wasn't
what made me get in the car, in fact, it all but kept me from
doing so."

"Why *did* you get into the car?"

"I—You're distracting me."

He arches a dark brow. "I'm distracting you?"

"It's not your money either, which you must have
thought about."

"I thought it was my hot body," he teases.

"It's not your money," I say, unwilling to let this topic
go for reasons that I can't define, yet still feel important.
"Actually, I think your money is part of my reservation.
Yes, I hate your money."

"And why is that, Mia?"

"You have to expect everyone wants it. You have to
expect I'll want it. You won't ever be real because you won't
ever believe I'll be real. Sex would be the only thing real
with you, which doesn't require a trip to the Hamptons."

He leans in and cups my face, his breath a warm tease
on my cheek before he kisses me, a deep, sexy slide of
tongue that leaves me panting as he says, "Is that real
enough for you?"

Too real, I think. There is something about Grayson that gets to me, that makes me do stupid things like getting into his car. "I need to leave."

I try to pull away from him, but he slides a hand under my hair and holds me to him. "Mia," he says softly.

"Grayson." My hand has planted itself on the hard wall of his chest. "I want you. I don't think I could hide that very well but if this is just fucking, can we just do that? Then I'll go back to work and you'll go back to being king of the world without me?"

He kisses me again, and my God, the man can kiss, and he smells all woodsy and spicy and addictive. "Don't move," he orders softly before he releases me and then exits the car. I assume he's going inside to cancel the chopper, but suddenly he's opening my door and squatting beside me.

"What are you doing?" I ask.

"Getting you out of here," he says, reaching across me for my seatbelt, his arm brushing my breast in the process, and the tightening of my nipples radiates straight to my sex.

He freezes a moment and I sense a hunger in him, which only serves to stir more hunger in me. He unclips my seatbelt and pulls me to my feet, shutting the door and then leaning me against it, his big body framing mine. His hands on my hips. "I don't bring women to the Hamptons or my apartment," he says. "And yes, I am going to fuck you, Mia, before and after you try my favorite pizza spot *in the Hamptons*." He brushes a strand of hair from my eyes. "If you come with me." He releases me and steps back, offering me his hand and a choice as he does.

I don't ask him to explain. Maybe he just wants to keep our fling private. I *am* an employee of his company. Or maybe there's more to this. I'm not sure, but when I look into his eyes, the connection we share is real and I have this sense that Grayson Bennett needs something real in his life, if only for right now. I press my hand to his and when it closes down on mine, some part of me knows that this night and this man are about to forever change me.

Grayson walks me to him and then puts us both in motion. "Have you ever been to the Hamptons?" he asks.

"No. Have you ever been to Brooklyn?"

He laughs a low, deep, sexy laugh I feel from head to toe. "I know Brooklyn better than you might think."

"You own half of it, right?"

"I do not," he says, opening the door for me to enter the building, "in fact own anything in Brooklyn."

I enter the building, where a small waiting area is my destination with a dozen empty seats and glass doors leading to, I assume, the chopper. Grayson joins me, taking my hand again, his opposite hand lifting to the solo, thirty-something man behind a counter. "Jesse." The greeting is light, genuine, and without airs.

"It'll be five minutes, Grayson," Jesse replies, casual and comfortable, even friendly, with Grayson. He doesn't act like Grayson is a billionaire with an ego.

Grayson nods to the other man and turns to face me, returning to our prior conversation. "I don't own half of Brooklyn, however, I do have a close friend, and business associate who grew up in Brooklyn a few streets from where you grew up."

"And you know this because you looked at my HR file?"

"Yes, Mia," he confirms. "I looked at your HR file."

"I guess that's fair. I googled you. I probably know more about you than you do about me now."

"You know what I allow to be known."

"Because nothing is real."

His hands come down on my hips and he pulls me to him. "Be real with me, Mia, and I'll be real with you."

"I dare you to mean those words or not," I amend, pulling back to look at him. "I don't have any expectations." It hits me that he's made me promises but I have made him none. "If this is pizza and a fuck, then it's pizza and a fuck and no one will ever know but you and me. That's as real as it gets."

He cups my face. "I can already tell you that that's not real enough, but it's a start." He kisses me and once again I'm breathless.

Our lips are still lingering together when someone clears their throat and Grayson smiles. "Let's go eat that pizza." He takes my hand and as we walk toward the exit, one word stays in my mind: Real. It's a word that matters to him. It's a word that matters to me.

A few minutes later when he helps me into the chopper and we buckle up, I go back to the word "real." There's a real possibility I'm in over my head with this man, and yet, I can't seem to care. The chopper door is still open, and I know only one thing with certainty: I'm not leaving and that's as real as it gets.

CHAPTER TWENTY-SEVEN

Mia

The present

It's not long before Eric and Davis are back at the house. Somehow Eric manages to not only contact his ex-SEAL buddy who he's hired to help with the Ri situation, but he manages to get Adam to the Hamptons in rapid, nearly impossible, speed.

Adam turns out to be tall, good looking and in his mid-thirties, with dark, wavy hair. "Adam is an expert of disguise," Eric says as we all gather around the kitchen island. "That's his thing. He can get anywhere and no one will know it's him."

I wonder what Adam's thing was, but I assume for a SEAL that could just be his ability to kill and protect. It's a bit disconcerting how comforting that is right about now, but then, my gut is screaming with a warning. We're wading in knee-deep quicksand, still moving, but there's the very real possibility that we're already trapped and going under but don't know it yet. "Walker Security is a diverse, skilled group," Adam says, pulling me back into the moment as he responds to something Grayson has asked about Adam's employer. "Mia," Adam says, "I need you to tell me about the dynamic between you and Ri."

Grayson's displeasure cuts through the air and I have no doubt every person in this house feels the blade. "He wants to fuck her for obvious reasons, but as an added plus, he'd fuck me at the same time."

Tension curls in my belly. This isn't a topic I enjoy sharing, but it's necessary. "He tried to kiss me recently," I say. "I kneed him. Hard. Really hard. He's pretty bitter." I go on to run through the details of Ri finding out that I'm looking for a job and the Monday meeting.

Adam listens without much input and for the most part, Eric and Davis simply take it all in as well. They're all thoughtful, attentive, intelligent people who will all have opinions, some of which I won't agree with and some that I will. I prepare myself for the varied opinions, but Adam guides the conversation in an unexpected direction. "We already have a female from our team ready to stay at your apartment tonight," he says. "With Ri showing interest in you, Mia, I suggest we have me play the boyfriend, and I can hang out with our Mia double at your place."

"No," I say, rejecting that idea. "Ri has to think he has a chance to turn me or he'll go at Grayson ten times harder."

"Mia, damn it," Grayson says, his voice low, guttural.

I turn to him, my hand on his chest. "Hear me out. He feels like I'm a weapon. Let him keep that weapon while you knock his legs out from underneath him."

"At the risk of being pummeled," Eric says, "I agree. We'll watch her, Grayson. We'll wire her. We'll keep her with you as much as possible."

"Just make it count," I say, focused on Grayson. "Use me to take him out before he takes you out."

Grayson pulls me to him, ignoring the rest of the room. "I will. You can count on it."

He says those words so damn vehemently I want to cheer. His focus is no longer on getting me out of town. It's on ending this, on beating Ri once and for all. I push to my toes to give Grayson a quick kiss, but he cups the back of my head and slants his mouth over mine in a sultry, hot kiss that has Eric clearing his throat. "All right then. Time for us to head to the chopper service."

As in all of us, since Eric and Davis missed their original departure time. Grayson reluctantly turns his attention to the room, his gaze on Adam. "Whatever it takes, he goes down. You understand?"

"Quite well," Adam states. "Eric made that point in crystal clear terms."

"Make sure you make it to your team," Grayson replies. "Whatever it takes."

"Perhaps we should talk outside," Adam states.

"You can ride with me and Eric to the airport," Grayson states, kissing me. "Ride with Davis, baby."

I don't like the way this is going down, but I'm not going to push. Grayson doesn't like what Ri is making him become. I'll give him the space he needs to handle this without worrying about how I'll react. He'll tell me what he did later when he's ready. "What about my car?"

"I have another female agent handling it," Adam states. "We have you covered." He looks at Grayson, who motions him forward. It's clear that right now Grayson is focused and he wants action.

Grayson and Adam head toward the door. Eric stands his ground and leans on the island across from me. "Selfless, beautiful, and in love. You're what he needs. I might even fucking love you myself, that's how much I believe he needed you." He pushes off the island and follows Grayson and Adam toward the door.

Davis steps in front of me. "I don't love you, but I like you."

I laugh. "Right. You like me, but you accused me of being up to no good."

"I had to push you and then look into your eyes and see what there was to see."

"And what did you see?"

"His future wife."

Those words stay with me as we head to Davis's rental and with good reason. Grayson asked me to come home, but he didn't give me my ring back. By the time I'm in the passenger seat of the sedan, Davis is in the driver's seat. He shuts the door and then sits there a minute. "He'll ask again."

The words shock me and I turn to look at him. "What?"

"I'm a damn good attorney for a reason. I hit a nerve with the future wife thing. He'll ask again."

I inhale and shake my head, but I say nothing else. The only words that matter are the ones between me and Grayson, which are still too few. Thankfully Davis has never been a man of many words and he is, in fact, good at reading people. He leaves me to my thoughts, which include a reply to that talk about flaws that keeps bothering me.

The ride is short, though, and we pull through a private gate to park at a smaller building. The minute Davis kills the engine, Grayson is at my door, opening it, and pulling me to my feet, molding me close. "How was your talk?" I ask.

"Productive. Unfortunately, we need to meet a couple of Adam's team at the apartment when we get home."

"*Home*," I say. "I love that word."

"I'm glad you do, baby." He kisses me. "Come on." He takes my hand and guides me toward the chopper.

I have déjà vu about ten times over in the next five minutes. This place, the Sunday night return to the city, Grayson helping me into the chopper, his hand at my waist, us side by side in leather seats, familiar seats. And then, Grayson reaches over me and connects my seatbelt, and I flash back to that first Sunday again when he'd done the same thing: *Now you go home with me*, he'd said. Grayson's lips hint at a curve, his green eyes alight with memories, and he lets me know that he's thinking the same thing I am by saying, "Now you go home with me," but he adds, "Now *we* go home."

My hand goes to his jaw, and suddenly, the ring doesn't matter. What matters is what comes next. "Now we go home," I say.

CHAPTER TWENTY-EIGHT

Mia

Once we land in the city, Grayson and I part ways with the rest of the men and head to his Porsche. The minute I bring it into view, I smile. "You finally got the sapphire blue you wanted," I say, "and the very idea that you denied yourself because you had a car and didn't need another, is part of your appeal. You could do everything in excess, but you don't."

"The only thing I need in excess is you, baby," he says, clicking the door lock and pulling me to him to give me a quick kiss. His voice lowers and he repeats, "Just you," in a rougher, affected voice that has me all kinds of equally affected.

"Me, too," I say. "You. Just you."

He strokes my hair and then opens the door for me. It would probably be silly to most people, but I missed little moments like this one in such a huge way. I mean, it's just a door, but it's so much more. Once Grayson has sealed me inside the Porsche and has joined me, we just sit there for a moment and stare at each other until we both start smiling. I'm going home. That's what we're both thinking. I know it. He knows it. "Come here," he orders, his hand sliding under my hair to my neck as he leans over to kiss me and whispers, "Mia."

"Grayson," I murmur.

We both smile again and I swear I'm not sure I really smiled at all this past year, not a real smile as I have with him this weekend. Grayson settles back behind the wheel and cranks the engine, all kinds of masculine perfection as he does. "I really did miss your obsession with Porsche," I declare.

He casts me a sideways look. "You love Porsche, too."

"I love you behind the wheel of a Porsche," I say. "You make the car look good."

"*You* make the car look good, baby." He winks, backs up, and soon we're on the road with only a short drive ahead of us to be home. My hot man is a billionaire and doesn't act like it in ways others with money do, but then, his father beat the word "humble" into his head.

I have the briefest flashback of the first time I met his father, an older version of Grayson, who'd stayed fit and handsome, which made the heart attack shocking. *I've been sitting in a coffee shop and he's shocked me by sitting down right in front of me.*

"You're dating my son."

"Yes," I say. "I am."

"But you work for the company."

"Do you want me to resign?"

"I hear you work very hard," he says.

"From Grayson?"

"No. Everyone."

"Harder than ever now. I don't want to seem like I'm riding his coattails. I didn't want to date him for that very reason but, well, I ran into him quite literally and it just— we happened."

"Are you after his money?"

"I hate his money," I say, as I had to Grayson. "I really hate his money."

He arches a brow. "Why?"

"Because you have to ask me that question. Because he has to ask that question of everyone around him. I didn't think we could be real for that reason. I didn't think he could be real with anyone."

His lips quirk. "His mother hated my money. She really hated my money. Did you know that?"

"Grayson told me. He's told me a lot about his mother. He loved her very much."

"And she loved him very much. Do you love Grayson?"

"Yes. Very much."

"Then why are you hiding your relationship?"

"I can't be the girl who slept her way to the top."

"Then don't be. Win and win big. No one can question you if you do that, but they will question you and create rumors about you and my son. I had to find out from Leslie. I'll tell you what I'm going to tell Grayson. Own it. Deal with it. I won't give you special treatment and neither will Grayson. I didn't give him special treatment."

"I don't want special treatment."

"Good." He winks. "I suspect I'll see you soon, Mia."

He gets up and leaves.

"Mia?"

I blink and glance at Grayson who's halted us at a stoplight. "Yes?"

"Where were you right now?" Grayson asks.

"I was remembering the day your father outed us."

He laughs. "Ah, yes. You called me in a panic."

"We'd only been seeing each other for six weeks and he had me confessing love before I even told you. And he showed up at the apartment that night and told you I said I loved you."

"And then I told you that I loved you." He winks like his father had that day in the coffee shop, so like him it's scary.

"How did he have a heart attack?" I ask. "He was so fit."

"He had a heart defect they said he probably had his entire life."

"Did you get checked?"

"It's not an inherited condition."

"Still, can you please just get checked?"

He takes my hand and kisses it. "I'm fine."

His cellphone rings, forcing me to bank this topic for now as Eric's number flashes across his dash. Grayson releases me and punches the Bluetooth button. "We're three minutes away," Grayson answers.

"I'm in your lobby," he says. "Just a heads up that Adam has two men with him, one of whom is Blake Walker, one of the three Walkers who owns Walker Security. He's also considered one of the best hackers in the world, and I mean that quite literally. He's already been digging around."

"And?" I prod quickly.

"That's all I know," Eric says. "I was just given this information."

"We'll see you in a few," Grayson says and disconnects as we approach the gorgeous glass high-rise that is our destination. "If this Blake Walker can't prove I'm being set up, I don't know who can," he says, pulling us into the parking garage and it's not long until we're parked in his private space. "There has to be a trail he can follow." He opens his door to get out and I forget about Blake. Right now, I'm about to be home for the first time in a year and some part of me just needs to know that's what it still feels like—home. I want to know that we still feel like us when we walk in the door.

I don't wait for Grayson to help me out of the car. I get out and he meets me on my side. "Have you changed anything at the apartment?"

"Everything is as you left it, waiting for you to return." He strokes my hair out of my eyes, his touch sending a shiver down my spine. "Just like I was."

"I really do wish that we were doing this alone."

"We'll be alone soon. We'll be in our bed again soon." And with that promise, he laces the fingers of one of his hands with mine, and folds our elbows, aligning our hips and setting us in motion. That silly question of this feeling like home fades. Home is Grayson, not the apartment, and if this is what being flawed feels like, flawed feels pretty damn perfect.

CHAPTER TWENTY-NINE

Mia

Eric, Davis, Adam, and two men he introduces as Blake and Asher, wait for us at the elevator on our floor. Blake and Asher are casual in jeans and Walker Security T-shirts, and they both have long hair tied at the nape, only Blake has dark hair and no obvious ink while Asher has blond hair and double tattooed sleeves.

"Let's head inside," Grayson says, motioning toward the apartment and my stomach flutters with the realization that this is it. The moment where Grayson and I come full circle.

He leads me forward and when we reach the door, he pulls me in front of him and surprises me by pressing a key into my hand. I look down to find my old pink keychain. It's my key. Emotion and heat overwhelm me to such a degree that my hand trembles as I lift it. Grayson must notice, as he covers my hand with his and helps me open the door.

Together.

We open it together.

As it should be, I think.

I step into the foyer, which is a square room with dark wood floors and ivory walls and an ivory low-to-the-ground table in the center with a couple dozen teardrop lights dangling above it. Grayson steps to my side and his arm slides around my shoulders. He ignores the rest of the crowd and walks me forward under an archway and into the stunning living room, which is a wide open space that seems to sit on the ocean during the day and at night, as is the present case, a sea of stars and city lights.

To my right is a grand piano, which Grayson has played since he was a child, while the center of the room is set with distinction by a cream-colored rug. The two couches facing each other are a deep, gorgeous blue that we'd picked together only a few months after I'd moved in. He'd wanted the house to be ours. He'd wanted me to feel this was my place, not just his. I'd just wanted him, but he'd been right. Making choices together had made me feel like this was our place and it still does.

Grayson steps behind me, his hands on my shoulders, his lips near my ear. "I have not fucked you on those couches in far too long."

I smile and my cheeks are downright flushed, I am certain, as Eric and the masses join us. Eric and Grayson share a look and without words, they decide on the dining room table, directly to our right, for our meeting which accommodates twelve and offers plenty of room. We all sit down at the long ivory table, more teardrop lights above it and us. Grayson sits in the center of me and Eric on one side, with Davis by Eric. While Blake, Asher, and Adam sit across from us.

"I'm going to hand the update over to Blake," Adam says. "Not only is he the boss, he and Asher are badass hackers, but first, Mia, is there anything our agents need to know? What is your morning routine?"

"I run at five. I leave my house at seven." My eyes go wide. "I have no clothes for work tomorrow."

"We can handle that," Adam says. "What do you need? I'll have it here in the morning."

"Everything," Grayson says. "Anyway you can make that happen, make it happen."

"We can do that," Adam says. "For the morning, though, let's keep the items limited and discreet." I give him a list that he writes down before he adds, "I'll be here at six in the morning. And that's all I need. I'll turn this over to Blake and Asher, who as I said, are expert hackers."

"Blake makes me look like an amateur," Asher says. "And I'm not amateur."

"Asher's damn good," Blake says. "But hacking is like a second skin to me. Asher is heading up the dive into your electronics, looking for those betraying you. I'm dealing with Ri."

"And?" Eric prods. "What do we know so far?"

"The electronic trail is too clean," Blake says. "Someone is wiping it, someone good."

"Which confirms that this is a well thought out, calculated hit," Grayson assumes.

"Exactly," Blake says. "But they've made mistakes and when I have more than two hours, as I just had, to find the problems, I'll find them."

"Mitch is a problem," I say. "He's one of Grayson's employees."

"We have eyes on him," Adam says.

"Physically and electronically," Asher adds.

"But you have nothing yet," I say.

Blake's piercing brown stare meets mine. "We will."

"You can't know that," I say. "I need to know what I can get from Ri that ends this for Grayson."

Grayson's hand comes down on my knee and he squeezes. "Answer that knowing that she is all that matters to me."

Blake's eyes meet Grayson's. "As is my wife, and she is an ex-FBI agent who works for Walker. I understand where you're coming from." He looks between us. "We'll wire Mia. Adam filled me in on what happened. I doubt that you will get Ri to admit to setting up Grayson. A sudden change of attitude on your part, Mia, will be suspicious, but getting him to talk trash about Grayson is helpful."

"That's not going to do much of anything," I argue. "I'm a criminal attorney, remember?"

"I'm going to give you a couple of bugs to plant in his office and around the offices in general," Blake says, eyeing Grayson. "We're going inside your offices and bugging them as well. We're starting here locally and we'll expand based on where our initial research takes us." He refocuses on me. "Things you can get that help us: electronic devices and documents."

"I don't like this," Grayson says. "Mia could be placed in danger." He looks at me. "Just go. Convince Ri everything is fine. Let him talk you into staying and then just work, close the case you're on because that's the right move for your client. Leave the rest to the professionals."

"I'll be careful," I promise. "But I can easily place a few bugs. I can do this, Grayson. Let me do this for you, for us. For your staff."

"I'm going to be a stone's throw away," Asher says. "There won't be a moment that we aren't within her reach if she needs us."

Grayson starts tapping the table and then he stands, leaving everyone at the table. I glance over my shoulder to find him crossing the living room, toward the wall of windows. He's effectively told our audience he's done with everyone but me. Blake fixes me in an unaffected stare. "We'll leave you two to hash this out. Adam will be here in the morning. I'll call personally if we find out anything new. I plan to work all night."

"As do we all," Asher chimes in.

"I have a few questions," Eric says. "Can we continue this elsewhere?"

"Yes," Davis says. "Agreed. I have questions as well."

Blake nods and we all stand up. I walk them all to the door and Eric holds back to talk to me. "You okay?"

"Only when I know he's free of this."

"Agreed. Call me if you need me." He leaves and I lock the door.

I don't linger or contemplate what to say to Grayson. I'll know when I'm with him. I exit the foyer and find him still at the window, radiating dark, hard emotions and I am determined to make the man I love feel something other than those things; I want him to feel me and us.

CHAPTER THIRTY

Mia

Right when I would join Grayson at the living room window, there's a knock on the front door behind me. Obviously, it's one of the men that just left, most likely Eric and most likely he left something behind. Eager to be alone with Grayson, I turn back to the door and hit the camera button beside it to find Blake Walker waiting on the other side, and my heart races with the idea that he might have received some sort of news about the plot against Grayson.

I quickly open the door and he hands me a card. "In case you need me. That has my cellphone on it."

"Right." I don't feel relief. I feel disappointment. I want news. I want answers. "Thank you," I add.

He must read my reaction. "We'll make this go away," he promises. "When you set someone up for a crime, as Ri is doing to Grayson, you commit a crime yourself. Ri will pay for his jealousy and competitiveness going too far." He speaks with a confidence that I welcome. We need someone strong behind us right now and I do believe Blake Walker and his team are good additions to our efforts to shut down Ri. I hope Grayson feels the same and I urgently want to find out.

"*Thank you,*" I repeat but this time there's force behind the words.

His eyes narrow on mine as if he's looking for the same confidence in me that he's showing in himself. "I'll update you before bed." With that, he turns away.

I quickly shut the door and lock up again, stuffing his card into my pocket before I rush toward the living room. The minute I pass through the archway, my gaze seeks out Grayson but he's no longer by the window. The patio door is open, obviously his way of inviting me to join him. I close the space between me and that door, exiting the apartment, only to have Grayson grab me from the left. In a blink, I'm against the glass door and he's pressed close.

"You will not put yourself in the middle of this," he orders, his voice rough, his handsome face all hard lines and shadows, his fingers tangling in my hair and not gently. "I agreed to you going back for one reason: It buys me time to destroy him and that's for me to do, not you. You go. You convince him you're still there to stay and that's all."

"Yes, but—"

"No buts, Mia, That's all you do. The end. Do not argue."

"Grayson," I plead, but his mouth comes down on mine and his tongue drives away my objections, each stroke a demand that I cannot turn down.

"Nothing else," he says when his lips part from mine. "Do you understand me?"

Somehow after that kiss and with his perfect body pressed close, I manage a coherent reply. "Everyone in that room believes you need me."

"And they were right. I do need you. I've been quite clear on that point, which is why I'm protecting you. Anyone who will go as far as Ri is going over jealousy could be capable of more. You could get hurt and I'm not letting that happen."

"So could you. We protect each other."

"Mia—"

"Grayson—"

"You will not fight me on this," he says. "You will not win, so don't even try."

His voice is pure steel, the heavy-handedness of his mood is out of character for him, and to such an extreme that he turns me to face the glass, forcing me to catch myself on my hands. His legs cage mine, his hands shackling my hips, his lips at my ear. "You will not win." His hand slides upward and he cups my breast. "You will do as I say."

I cup his hand where it's covering my breast, and he squeezes while I manage to process the fact that he's not himself. He's lost his father. He's lost me. He can't lose me again. That's where this is coming from and I know that I can fight with him later if need be, debate with him, and we can make decisions together, but what he needs right now is agreement. "I'm not going to do anything we don't agree on, Grayson. I won't."

"You're right." He pulls my shirt over my head. "You won't." And before I even know it's happened, my bra is unhooked too. He drags me to him, cradling my body to his harder one to rid me of my bra completely, his hands cupping my breast, fingers closing down on my nipple. "And I won't change my mind."

I moan with the sensations rocking my body, spikes of pleasure blossoming from my nipples straight to my sex. "I'm going to try, though," I pant out. "You know that."

He leans me forward again, pressing my hands to the wall by my head. "Don't try, Mia. It takes away time we can just be here, home, together." He slides to my side, his leg still at the back of my knees, caging me, the lean of my body forcing my hands to stay put.

"I was never your submissive, Grayson," I remind him. "I'm not starting now."

"No?" he demands, unsnapping my jeans, and dragging the zipper down. "Are you sure about that? I seem to remember plenty of submissive moments." He moves behind me and drags my pants down.

"Sex doesn't count," I pant out, trying to look over my shoulder, only to have him palm my backside and then give it a hard smack.

"Grayson!" I yelp. "We don't do this like that."

"Now we do," he promises, shoving my pants down further and then lifting me and I don't know how he manages it, but in about thirty seconds, I'm also naked from the waist down. He smacks my backside again, and heat rushes through me.

"Grayson," I bite out this time. "I thought you didn't spank me out of anger?"

"Tonight, I do." He leans in close, near my ear again. "Did it hurt?"

"No," I whisper. "Not hurt. You know you didn't hurt me."

"Then what's the problem?" He spanks me again and I arch into the touch.

"The problem," I hiss, "is you're mad and I'm aroused right now and I shouldn't be."

"No," he says, easing back to my side, and squeezing my cheek, his free hand on my belly, "you shouldn't be. That defeats the purpose of a spanking when I'm this mad at you." His hand slides between my legs, fingers sliding along the wet seam of my sex. "You will not come."

"I'm pretty sure that I am, in fact, going to come if your fingers stay where they're at right now and you spank me again."

He cups my sex and spanks me again. I gasp, arching into the palm now back to squeezing my ass, and then into the one cupping my sex. "Grayson," I whisper, though I have no idea what I'm asking for. "Can you please—"

His fingers slide inside me, his lips at my ear. "Please what, baby?" The words are soft, seductive, but that edge, his anger, is not gone. It's sharp. It's moody and present. It's a wedge between us and I can't take it.

"I'm just trying to protect you," I whisper. "The way I should have before."

His fingers slide out of me and he turns me to face him, those green, tormented eyes fixed on me. "Protect me by trusting me this time. Trust me that he's dangerous. Trust me to protect you and us."

"I do," I whisper. "I just—"

"Don't finish that sentence, baby. Not right now." He cups my face. "Just be here."

My hands go to his hands. "I am. I've never been anywhere but here."

His mouth crashes down on mine and the taste of him explodes on my tongue: torment, fear, pain, loss, hunger, *need*. He needs so much and he has hurt so much and I can't do anything to add to those feelings. I just don't know how to do that but I'll decide with him. That's the only way this works. He scoops me up and starts walking. I'm naked in his arms while he is fully dressed and I have this sense of being willingly vulnerable with this man. I would do anything with him and anything for him.

CHAPTER THIRTY-ONE

Mia

Grayson settles me on one of the soft navy-blue couches, the cushion absorbing my weight, while Grayson's big body frames mine, even as he pulls his shirt over his head and tosses it. "You," he says, "will listen to me." He doesn't give me time to reply, by obvious intent. He kisses me, licking me into that submission we both know he can get from me if he so pleases because Grayson's subtle demand for power is not so subtle when we're naked.

One of his hand slides under my backside, while the other covers my breast. He's not even undressed yet and I'm wet, wanting, and in need of him, but I know him. I know I will not be easily sated. I know the darker side of Grayson that no one else does, and in his present mood, he'll deny me until I'm downright desperate. "Don't move," he orders when his mouth parts from mine, but *he* moves. He lifts his body off of mine and then suddenly I'm on my stomach. He's turned me over and before I can even gasp, I'm not just on my stomach, he's dragging me to my elbows and knees. "Down," he says, his hand on my back and I get it and him. He needs control right now. He feels like I'm taking it. I *have* taken it.

I sink as low as this position allows me.

He's on his knees beside me, his hand caressing a slow path up and down my spine. "God, I missed you, Mia," he says, but there's a vibration in his tone I do not like.

"Why do you say that like it pisses you off?"

"Wanting you isn't what pisses me off and you know it." He stands up and I can hear him begin to undress, while he's left me here submissive, vulnerable, and willing. Because I do know why he's angry. He's angry that I left. He's mad that I misjudged him and while he'd denied those feelings back in the Hamptons, he's not denying them now. He needs my submission now and I'll give it to him, but I always did. He has always been the one person that I would dare to do anything with. He's always been that man for me, the *only* man for me.

I trust him.

I trust him completely.

My God, how did I let myself forget that? But I know in this moment exactly how. I know the flaw, my flaw, maybe *our* flaw. He sits down behind me on the couch, but I don't wait for what comes next. I need to talk to him, I need to touch him. I sit up and twist around to straddle him and all his hard, naked perfection, his erection thick at my bottom. "I know what you wanted and needed right now, but I need to say something to you. I trust you," I say, my hands on his shoulders but he doesn't touch me.

"Are you sure about that, Mia? Because you're on my lap right now. You don't seem to even trust me like this, naked."

"No, that's what I'm telling you. When I was laying there I thought: I trust him. How did this happen? How did we get here? And then it hit me. I trust you completely. I trusted you completely and the idea that I could trust that much, and find that woman pressed against you, I just— that was such a deep wound. Don't you see?"

"No, Mia, I don't. Because what happened didn't feel like trust."

My lashes lower with his anger and I force aside a moment when I want to shut down, which was exactly where I went wrong with our breakup and exactly why I admit, "I shut down. It was the only way to protect myself. That was the flaw that was really perfection. I trusted you so completely that I didn't know how to survive the wound."

"You didn't fully trust me or you wouldn't have needed to shut down."

"I did. I swear to you, Grayson. I did."

"I don't know what to do with that, Mia. You want a reason to distrust me?"

"I loved you to the point that your betrayal felt like it would end me. I can't be with you if you're going to resent me. I can't be with you if you don't think I deserve everything again. You just—I just need you to know that maybe I loved *too* much." I try to move away but he catches me, his hand on my hip and the back of my head.

"Maybe you didn't love me enough," he says. "Maybe you didn't love me like I did you because I couldn't have left you."

"Loved?"

"You know I still love you."

"Maybe not enough." I try to move again and suddenly my stomach is not feeling well but Grayson holds me. "Let go. I feel sick. I need up."

"Stop, baby. Stop pulling away." He rests his forehead against mine. "I love you more than I love life itself. I'd say you know that, but obviously, you don't. Obviously, you *didn't.*"

"I did. It was my own insecurity that got us here. I told you that back in the Hamptons."

"How do we fix that? Did I do something to create it? Because if anyone knows I'm not perfect, it's you. I let you see everything. You made me be real, remember?"

"Real is good and I don't want you to stop being real even if that means being angry, but forgive me, okay? Because we can't do this if you can't."

"I'm angry at us both for letting it happen," he says, "not just you."

"Well then, yell at me, fuck me, do whatever it takes, but stop being angry."

"No yelling," he says, dragging my mouth to his. "Lots of fucking."

Our mouths collide and our tongues stroke long and deep, a frenzied rush of kissing, touching, and him lifting me to press the soft tip of his thick erection inside me. I gasp as he pulls me down and drives into me. We stay there, connected in the most intimate of ways, breathing together, wanting together, savoring each other until a crackle of electricity seems to snap between us and we're kissing again, our bodies swaying, grinding, swaying some more.

At some point, we move from that seductive emotional bond to one that borders on pure physicality. I lean back into his thrusts while his gaze rakes over my breasts, a hungry look on his handsome face. His fingers clamp down on my nipples, and with each push and pull of my body, sensations ripple along my nerve endings, tightening my sex, and I just need to be closer to him. I lean in again and our kisses become desperate. His hand squeezes my backside and then he gives me a hard smack that has me gasping and arching into his thrust.

"Oh, God," I breathe out because the man rocks my entire world in every way.

He reacts by rolling me to my back, and thrusts and pumps, his hand under my backside, lifting me into a deeper, harder, spot that has me shattering with no warning. I am just there, right *there,* in that perfect place, and my sex clenches around him. Grayson buries his face in my neck and he groans, this deep, sexy, groan and shudders into release.

For just a moment, he all but flattens on top of me, but then he rolls us to our sides, facing each other, fingers tenderly stroking my brow. "Don't leave again," he says. "You stay. We fight. We fuck."

"Yes," I whisper. "I stay. We fight. We fuck."

"Good. Then we need to talk, and we might need to fuck again when it's over."

"About Ri?"

"Yes, baby, about Ri."

CHAPTER THIRTY-TWO

Mia

Grayson shifts us and we both sit up on the couch, and then he's standing, taking me with him. I yelp as he scoops me up again, but I don't know why I'm surprised. The man is always carrying me around, but then we've been apart for a year. What is familiar is being reintroduced and in every way, it still feels perfect. He loves to carry me around and I love when he does. A short walk later, I'm on the counter in our stunning bathroom with white tile trimmed by wood that matches the floors. Grayson walks to the bathroom door, reaches behind it and grabs a pair of pajama bottoms he pulls on, which reminds me of my robe that had once hung in the same spot.

"Remember this?" he asks, pulling that very robe from the hook.

"You never moved it?" I ask, surprised by just how much he'd kept his home my home.

He crosses to wrap the white silk around me. "It's been waiting on you, just like me," he says as I slip my arms into it.

"You tried to fuck me out of your system, though," I say, feeling the bite of that confession.

He strokes my cheek, cupping it to force my gaze to his. "Mia—"

"It's okay," I say, covering his hand. "I left. I left for a year. You're human. You needed what I wasn't here to give you."

"I needed *you*." His hands settle on my waist. "I can't change how I handled you leaving any more than you can change leaving. You were right in the living room. We need to move on. We need to look forward. I want you back here. I want you next to my side. I want you out of Ri's company."

"Me, too, on all counts. I have a case, though, a woman that I really want to help. I can't dump the case. She killed her abusive husband, but the trial date isn't for four months."

"You aren't staying there for four months." His hands move to my knees.

"I know," I say quickly. "I'm not suggesting that I do. I just hate deserting her. I'm passionate about her case. She was defending herself from a brutal attack and she shouldn't have been charged. It's wrong that she's going through this. She trusts me and if she follows me to Bennett, Ri could sue me and you."

"Ri won't be suing anyone when I'm done with him," he bites out, his voice low, tight. "Let's talk about what went wrong in that meeting tonight."

"You didn't like Blake or his team?"

"Not one of them brought up the possibility that Ri could have been having you followed and knows you've been with me this weekend."

"I'm sure that's assumed with all of the efforts to hide my present location."

"I don't like unspoken assumptions that impact your safety," he says.

"You really believe Ri is dangerous?"

"Yes. I do. If Blake's team shows up here in the morning and doesn't make me feel really damn good about you going to that meeting with Ri tomorrow, you're not going."

My hands cover his. "I know you're worried about me."

"Mia, do not fight me on this."

"I know you lost your father and I left, but I'm not leaving again. I won't be stupid. If I get a bad feeling, and you know I have good gut feelings, I'll just leave."

"If you can," he says. "That building is locked down by Ri's people, who were good enough to hide from a world class hacker like Blake Walker."

Nerves knot my belly. I'm starting to get nervous, but I have to do what I can to protect Grayson. "Okay. So what makes us feel good about me going in there tomorrow?"

"Nothing."

"Grayson," I plead. "I can buy you time. I can keep his guard down just by making him think nothing has changed. I don't have to play detective."

"We'll both know in the morning when Blake's team shows up. Fair enough?"

"As long as you haven't made up your mind already," I agree.

"I do need to buy time, a few days to let our people work," he concedes. "And I do believe you suddenly quitting would put him on edge. He'd look for trouble, but it's not worth it if it puts you in danger. Agreed?"

"You going to jail for something you didn't do is not okay. I'm willing to take risks for you."

"You are, just by walking back into that building and that's more than I want you to do."

"But you will," I press.

His jaw sets hard. "If I feel good about it in the morning." He lifts me off the counter and sets me in front of him. "How about some dinner?"

"Chinese?"

"Yes," he says. "Chinese."

"You do know I still haven't become domestic, right?" I tease. "We're going to live a life of takeout in between the meals Leslie makes us."

"I can live with a life of takeout," he assures me, his green eyes lighting with laughter that I'm pleased to see return. He kisses my temple. "Now if I can just find my phone." He turns me toward the door and smacks my backside. I yelp, but I'm smiling as I head to the bedroom, right up until the moment I reach the doorway. I stop there dead in my tracks and I stare at the room that was mine with Grayson, that is mine with Grayson *again*.

We decorated it together as well, picked out the navy headboard on the massive bed with chairs that match by the window. We love blue. We love this room. Grayson steps behind me, and his hands settle on my shoulders. "This is where you belong."

I rotate to face him. "With you is where I belong. I never felt at home at that apartment, but I tried. I thought I had to make it without you, so I tried."

"Like I tried, Mia, but in a different way. I needed our place to be a sanctuary when you returned, our home, and I promise you, I'll protect that always." His hand slides under my hair to my neck. "You fill all the empty places in this home. You fill all the empty places in me, and you're the only one who knows they exist. Because I trust you, Mia."

"Do you?" I challenge, "Because—"

"I thought you left me for Ri," he says. "As I stand here thinking about what you said in the living room, I understand it. I trusted you completely. I pulled back when I thought you betrayed me because to trust that much and be betrayed cuts deeper than any blade, but I'm not pulling back now or ever again. Me and you, forever." He leans in, kisses me and the touch of his lips, tender and yet possessive, sends a rush of heat and awareness through my body.

"You don't just belong with me," he says. "You belong *to* me, and Ri is going to know that before this is over." There is something in his voice, a lethal quality that gives me pause.

Despite my push for him to go on the attack, this is the first time I've been concerned that the remedy he plans could be worse than the crimes he's been wrongly accused of. I pull back to look at him. "What are you going to do, Grayson?"

"Whatever it takes to end Ri."

"End Ri?" I ask, because that tone again, that look in his eyes, worries me. "What does that mean?"

He lowers his mouth to mine and says, "It means he won't be at our wedding, baby." He seals that declaration with a kiss that is meant to silence my questions and it works. "And yes, I'm going to ask again. Once I know that I'm not dragging you to hell with me."

"I'll go anywhere with you," I promise.

"But I won't let you." He strokes my cheek. "Because that's love, Mia. I take care of you before me." He kisses me. "I'll order the food." He heads toward the bedroom door and I think about those words. He takes care of me over himself. I need to take care of him over myself, but the problem is, with Grayson there is loss and pain to consider. I can't make a stupid decision that leaves me dead and him destroyed. I can't sacrifice myself without taking him with me. And yet, I have to go meet with Ri tomorrow after Grayson has all but declared him a killer.

CHAPTER THIRTY-THREE

Grayson

I lay in the bed holding Mia, her back to my chest, my arm wrapped snugly around her, the electronic panels on the windows sealing out any ray of the new day surely upon us; the day Mia goes back to work with Ri. I tighten my grip on her and in this moment, I'm split between heaven and hell. Heaven is having her back here in my life, in our home, in our bed. Hell is letting her go back to work today. I don't trust Ri. And I know Mia, she's all heart and passion for those she cares about and I know damn well no matter what promise she makes me about protecting herself, she's going to be tempted to put me first. It's part of what makes her, her. It's part of what made losing her so damn painful. She loves with all her heart and you feel it as deeply as she gives it.

"You're awake," Mia says, and that voice, so sweet with the hint of a rasp, always undoes me, but then everything about this woman undoes me.

"I'm awake," I say softly, leaning in and kissing her neck. "You shouldn't be. It's still early."

She reaches for the remote and turns on the bedside light to a low glow before rolling around to face me, her hand settling on my cheek. "Please tell me you slept," she says. "Because I did. I did because I'm home with you."

My hand goes to her hip and I pull her to me. "It was the best night I've had since the last time you were home in our bed."

"You didn't sleep," she accuses, not accepting my attempt at avoidance any more than she ever did. I mean how many times in the early days of our relationship did this woman look at me when I gave her a cookie cutter answer and call me on it?

I have a brief flashback of sitting across from her sharing our first pizza and her asking me, *"Why are you thirty-five and still single if your mom and dad were so happily married?"*

"I don't believe in marriage."

She studies me a moment and then says, "I'm sorry."

I frown at the odd reply. "What?"

"Everyone thinks your kind of money makes everything better, but it really does come with complications, doesn't it?"

"Yes," I find myself admitting. "It does."

"I don't want your money or a ring. I don't want to be bought. I just want to be here, right now, in the moment. It's okay if you want to really be here with me, I don't expect anything from you, Grayson. I won't become a problem for you later." She lifts the slice of pizza in her hand. "And this is a pretty good moment. Best pizza ever."

"Grayson."

I blink Mia back into view.

"Where were you right now?" she asks.

"Still with you, baby. I was just thinking about how good you are at calling me on my bullshit, even from the very beginning. That first night over pizza."

"Mr. I don't believe in marriage because it means everyone wants my money," she says, proving she knows exactly what I'm referencing. She laughs and sobers quickly. "And for the most part, they do want your money and your success. Ri is successful and wealthy but it's not enough because it's not what you have. Honestly, once I saw the magnitude of how much people want and want and want from you, I don't know how you ever let me inside."

"You didn't give me any other choice," I say, stroking a strand of hair from her eyes. "You took me by storm, Mia, and you still do. Truthfully, it's a relief to have someone I trust, someone who really knows me. You're the only one who does."

"Eric knows you. You trust him."

"Not in the way I do you. Not with everything."

She sucks in air. "And then I left."

I pull her closer, driven by emotions only this woman drags from me. "You're here now. That's what matters, but Mia, *I cannot* lose you again. I was laying here thinking about how hard it's going to be for you to step back and let me handle this."

"I promised you—"

"I know, and I know you meant it, too, but I also know *you*, baby. You will want to protect me and you won't walk away from the chance. I can't be pissed at you for wanting to protect me."

"You were last night."

"No," I say. "You read me right. I was pissed about you leaving. I was pissed that Ri is putting us through this."

"And that I let him."

"You're human, Mia. I can forgive you if you can forgive me."

"That's the first time I think you actually said you'd forgive me."

"I forgive you. Forgive me."

"For what?" she asks.

"I did try to fuck you out of my system and I know you're going to think about that but I wasn't going to lie to you. I should have recoiled to lick my wounds. I should have fought harder."

"Okay, you can stop blaming yourself any minute now because I'm not blaming you."

"Let's make a pact right now. It's over. We're together. We're not going to place blame."

"And yet we're flawed."

"We *are* flawed, Mia, beautifully, perfectly flawed in the way all humans are flawed. Perfect is an impossible façade to maintain. Love me for my imperfections, not my perfection, because perfection isn't real, and real is what you wanted from me, right?"

"Yes," she says, her voice cracking, eyes watering. "That's exactly what I've always wanted from you."

I lean in, my hand on her head, my lips near hers. "You got it, baby. All of me, completely me. Now," I brush my lips over hers, "what are you going to do with me?"

My cellphone rings at that moment and we both groan. I try to pull away and she catches my hand and presses her cheek to mine, her lips at my ear. "Lick you all over."

Now I groan and if I could just let her make good on that promise, I would, but I can't. Not this morning. I pull back, kiss her thoroughly and roll away to grab my phone from the nightstand right as it stops ringing. I'm just checking caller ID to find Eric's number when he calls again. "Eric," I answer.

"We'll be there in half an hour. I just thought after you and Mia reunited you might need a wake-up call."

"I assure you that this is not a morning that makes me want to sleep. Stay in bed and fuck, yes, but Mia isn't going to let that happen."

Mia leans over me and calls out, "Morning, Eric," completely unfazed by the conversation—but then Eric is like a brother to her so why would she be?

Eric chuckles. "Morning, Mia," he calls out and she kisses my shoulder and rolls away, the bed shifting as she gets up and heads to the bathroom.

"I need to go," I say, realizing that I haven't finished my talk with Mia over today and time is ticking. "Mia and I need to talk before you get here."

"Understood." We disconnect and I walk into the bathroom to find the shower on and Mia inside.

I strip out of my pajama bottoms and don't even hesitate to join her. She turns to face me, naked, wet and beautiful but I'm not distracted. I pull her to me, turn her, and press her to the wall. "I will not let you go today if I don't feel good about the plan in place. You will not fight me on this. Promise me, Mia."

"I never fight with you unless we're alone and I'm not going to start now. I have no desire to end up dead. I'll listen to what you think."

"Good, and if I let you go, try baby, try with all your might to remember your promise. Let me handle, Ri. Walk away so you don't end up dead. Don't think about me behind bars. I do have a shit ton of money and resources so that's not going to happen. I promise you."

"You don't know what he has on you."

"Mia—"

"I promise," she says. "I do. I don't want to screw up and lose us again."

I cup her face. "Say it again."

"I promise. I don't want to—"

I kiss her and drag her with me under the water, wishing like hell I had time to fuck her this morning and she doesn't make my willpower any stronger. Her hand wraps the thick ridge of my now rock-hard cock. "I think I need to remind you just how right here with you I am, Grayson."

"Later, baby. We're about to have a houseful of people."

"I don't think this will take long." She goes down on her knees just outside the spray, and holy fuck, her tongue licks the water off my cock and then she's suckling and licking and pumping. I don't even try to maintain my willpower. I haven't had this woman's mouth on me in far too long. My hands go to her hair and I hold on perhaps too tightly but Mia has always liked that part of me that can't hold back with her, perhaps because she knows she's the only one that does that to me.

She sucks, and now I move with her, and she's right, it doesn't take long before I shudder with release, and she suckles me until it's over. When it is, she's made her point. She's back. We're back. And damn, it's good. Too good to let that fucking little bitch Ri get in the way again. And he did get in the way of me and Mia, and for that, he will pay like I have not ever made anyone pay.

CHAPTER THIRTY-FOUR

Grayson

I finish shaving and pull on the navy-blue suit jacket with a light blue pinstripe which Mia insisted I wear because it's her favorite. I stare at it in the mirror and only then do I admit just how much I missed the hell out of all the little things, like her choosing my suit, and I'm not sure I let myself admit just how much until now when she's back. I couldn't. I'd have lost my fucking mind and I was already hanging on a ledge and bloodied as it was.

The doorbell rings and she rushes out of the closet in a pair of sweats and a T-shirt with no bra, her nipples puckering from underneath. "My hair isn't dry," she says. "Damn it, I'm behind."

"You also aren't wearing a bra, so stay the hell here. Finish up. I want to talk to Blake anyway."

She looks down at her nipples and back up at me. "Do you really think I'd go out there like this?"

I cross the room and pull her to me. "I'm feeling a little territorial this morning."

"Why? You do remember what I just did to you, right?"

"With crystal clear clarity that will distract me frequently," I assure her. "But right now, I'm deciding if you go back to Ri or not."

Her eyes go wide. "Back to Ri?" Anger flares in her eyes. "Grayson, damn it—"

I kiss her soundly on the lips. "I'm sorry, baby. I told you. I'm feeling territorial this morning. I know you were never with him. I just need to get past today and get you back home with me."

Her hand flattens over my heart. "I'll be back home with you and not soon enough for me." She pushes to her toes and kisses me. "I'll wait here until you're ready for me and if you don't feel good about today, we'll figure out what to do."

I cover her wet hair with my hand and kiss her again, but this time, it's a deep, drink-her-in kiss. "I love you, baby," I say, knowing damn well she wants to fight me over today but she knows me enough to know that now isn't the time to do that. Mia was right when she said she saves our fights for private moments, and as the doorbell rings again, we're both reminded that this isn't one of them.

"I'll come get you," I say, releasing her and heading for the other room.

By the time I'm at the front door, tension is radiating like a pulse down my spine. I open the door and Eric arches a brow at my slow response but like Mia, he and I have a history and not just with each other, with Ri, too. We all went to school together for a year before Eric changed schools and then went into the military. Now, years after leaving his family fortune behind, Eric is my best friend, confidant, and damn near a billionaire, by his own making.

I back up and allow him to enter. Adam and a brunette female in a skirt and blouse follow with Blake on their heels. Blake stops to talk to me as I shut the door. The rest of the group follows Eric into the apartment. "Who's the woman?" I ask.

"My wife, Kara, who's ex-FBI. We arranged to have her sent to Ri's office as a temp today. She's reporting to Mia's floor and I promise you this, she's lethal. I was undercover when she met me. She thought I was the enemy and she drugged me and left me flat on my ass. Not a moment I'm proud of but the point is, she knows how to get the job done."

"Or you don't," I counter.

He laughs. "Fuck, man, you had to take the shot, right?"

"Had to," I assure him.

His eyes meet mine. "As an added bonus, you know that the thing I cherish most in this world is with your woman."

"Keep talking," I say.

"We can't know that Ri didn't have Mia followed. He could know she was with you this weekend. I couldn't send Mia in there without knowing I had someone who would kill for her within reach. And Kara would."

"How much risk do you think there is to Mia?"

"I dug up enough on Ri to know that he's capable of just about anything."

"Meaning what?"

"Meaning he didn't scrub his data as far back as he should have. Five years ago, he was communicating with a mob affiliate named Rosemond, a man whose people will kill, smear, wound, and repeat for the right price, and he was doing it to win a case. You don't use someone like that guy and not have a really nasty side yourself and you don't connect yourself to Rosemond and walk away. I don't trust Ri. I don't want Mia near him, and yes, I considered telling you to pull her out of this completely."

"But you aren't. Why?"

"Pulling her abruptly doesn't just get Ri's attention and get him accelerating his efforts to take you down. It places attention on her. I'm going to tell you a story I tell very few and while some might consider it a poorly timed story, I do not, and I'll explain why after I tell it. Before Kara, I was engaged. I was undercover and so was Whitney, my fiancée. The man, the leader of a drug cartel, not only figured out I was ATF, he figured out that Whitney was everything to me. He killed her and she bled out in my arms."

His confession punches me in the chest and I turn away from him, pressing my hand on the door, a reaction I wouldn't normally allow anyone to see, but, "Fuck, Blake," I murmur, forcing myself back off that wall and to face him. "Tell me you killed him."

"That's a long, complicated story, but do you get what I'm telling you?"

"If he believes she's back with me, he'll see her as a weapon to use against me. I'm crystal clear on the point you've made. You better fucking protect her."

"I will," he replies.

I look up to find Kara standing a few feet away. "I'll protect her," she says. "I need to talk to her and help her with the wire. I need to come up with a plan of action for every possible scenario and Adam is working as a janitor in the building. He'll be right there with us."

I have to let Mia go to Ri today and it's killing me, but I'll never be captive like this again. I turn to Blake. "Make this count. Let me repeat what I told Adam, just to be clear. End him. I don't mean dead. That's too good for him. I want him to self-destruct. I want him to lose everything."

"And he will," Blake promises, "but you need to be removed from the process. It can't be about you, and my reason is this: If he's in bed with these gangsters I've connected him to and you take him down, you hurt their bank account. You don't want to cut the head off a snake to watch it grow another. You get the two of them fighting and they forget about you."

I narrow my eyes at him. "Where are you going with this?"

"We make sure Ri pisses off Rosemond. While Ri is playing defense, we make sure law enforcement raids his office on a matter related to Rosemond and just happen to find proof he set you up."

"What proof?" I ask.

"That's the hole," Blake says. "We need proof."

"Adam and Kara will place bugs in and around his office," Blake says. "But the only one who may be able to get close enough to Ri, to get real proof, is Mia. We need to know what role you want her to play."

"Mia's going to do her job and keep Ri in his happy zone. You get the damn proof yourself. That's what I'm paying you for." I start walking, pissed off that he just suggested Mia put herself on the line at all after he just told me about Whitney being murdered. "You want to meet Mia, Kara, come now."

I don't wait on her. I keep tracking forward and when I reach the bedroom she's on my heels. "Whatever you think Blake just suggested," Kara says. "He didn't."

I turn to face her. "It sounded like he wants Mia to fuck her way to finding that proof for me."

"No," Kara says. "He just asked your decision on her involvement. Everyone is not you. Everyone doesn't put their woman before themselves. That you do only makes me want to help you and protect her all the more. Blake feels the same, I promise you."

"Protect Mia above all else. I don't care if I rot in jail for crimes I didn't commit. Do you understand me?"

"Yes," Kara says. "I do. I'll protect Mia. You have my word." Her eyes lift to my shoulder and I realize then that Mia has opened the door.

CHAPTER THIRTY-FIVE

Mia

Protect Mia at all costs.

Grayson's words linger in the air as I step to his side and face the woman who's in front of him, who I assume works for Blake Walker. "And I'd ask you to protect him over me at all costs," I say, my hand going to Grayson's arm, and just being able to touch him again is like heaven on earth. "I guess," I add, "that's called love, right?" I turn to Grayson, push to my toes and kiss him.

He pulls me to his hip and stares down at me. "Most definitely love," he says, his voice low gravely, affected, and then without looking away he adds, "This is Kara, Blake's wife, and an ex-FBI agent who will be undercover as a temp in Ri's office today."

"Kara," I say, reluctantly pulling away from Grayson to turn and face her before offering her my hand. "Nice to meet you."

"A great pleasure to meet you, Mia. And right now, I need to get you wired." She indicates a roller bag she's grabbed on the heels of following me. "I have your clothes, as well. Hopefully, I chose well." She looks at Grayson. "Can Mia and I have a few minutes?"

"As long as you don't plan to corrupt her into doing something stupid," he replies dryly.

I give Grayson a gentle nudge. "I'm not that corruptible," I say.

"No," he says, "that's not the problem."

"What does that mean?"

"I'll just go on into the bedroom," Kara says, "if that's okay?"

"Of course," I say, stepping aside to allow her to enter, and even as she disappears I step in front of Grayson. "What did that mean?"

His hands come down on my arms and he drags me to him. "You have nothing to prove, you having nothing to repent with me. Don't go in there with Ri trying to make something up to me."

The words hit a nerve that I didn't know existed. He's right. I do want to make up for leaving him. I left him after his father died. "I'll be smart."

"Woman," he bites out. "That is not a reply I like. We had this conversation. You're going to want to protect me. Resist."

"You're letting me go. That must mean that Blake satisfied your expectations this morning."

"He brought up every concern I had and then some."

"And then some?"

He caresses my cheek. "They know what they're doing or I wouldn't be letting you go. You know that." He turns me to the door. "Go talk to Kara. I need you to know how to protect yourself while you're there today and I want to talk to Blake about how they're monitoring you while you're there." He smacks my backside and while that would normally send an erotic chill up my spine, it doesn't.

I suddenly want this day over with more than ever.

That gets me moving and I hurry back into the bedroom to find Kara standing by the bed where she's opened the suitcase she's used for my things, that isn't mine at all, and pulled out the three outfits she brought me. Grayson shuts the bedroom door for us behind me and I mentally choose the basic black skirt and royal blue blouse to wear today. I hate that I do it because Ri complimented me on that blouse, but today is all about making him feel that I'm team Ri without going overboard and raising suspicions.

"Let's get you dressed and wired first," Kara says, her hands settling at her hips. "I just need you right here in front of me and if you don't mind, in only your bra and panties. Sorry, I know you don't know me but I need to get this right and fast."

I laugh. "If I had those things on, that would be fine," I say, "but I don't."

She laughs. "Those are the best mornings. I brought you basic stuff, including those items, most of your bathroom toiletries, but not much else. I had to be discreet. I literally packed it in a duffle that I dropped out of your back window."

"Talk about resourceful," I say.

"But not early enough." She glances at her watch. "We're pushing it for both of us to get there."

A few minutes later, Kara's made the process quick and painless, and I'm fully dressed, working on makeup and hair in the bathroom with the supplies she's brought me. "Okay," she says, standing at the sink close to me while I work, "I need your phone. I'm going to put a collection of numbers in it. I'm first and Adam's second because we're closest in the building with you. I'm setting up a group message on your phone. Use it if you're in trouble so we all know at once."

They're worried. I'm worried. "How likely is it that Ri knows I was with Grayson this weekend?" I ask, turning to face her with Grayson's concerns on my mind.

"If he had you followed when you first split with Grayson I wouldn't assume that would continue. You stayed away from Grayson too long for him to think that you'd suddenly return. However, he's trying to take down Grayson. He could be paranoid."

The part about me staying away from Grayson feels pretty crappy. God. Why did I stay away? "Let's assume he knows and he confronts me. I don't have a story or an excuse. I need one." I press fingers to my temple. "Think, Mia." I look at her. "I have nothing."

"Tell him you invested money through Grayson but he wouldn't pay you out without seeing you and it was a packaged deal with a set end date. That way he can't check it. An agreement between you and Grayson. Be angry about it. That's your chance to be on team Ri."

"That's brilliant."

"We used it in another case so I'm not thinking on the fly. A group of us came up with it in a similar situation. That's the benefit of experience. Last thing. If you end up in trouble, go to the most public place and wait on me. The reception area. The lobby. Even an elevator instead of the stairs, but the elevator can be unpredictable for a fast escape. If you need fast, take fast, but remember there are cameras in the elevator that we've tapped into. There are no cameras in the stairwells and that's a hard area to place hidden cameras that matter. It's too many spaces in one path."

I take it all in and in a few minutes, I have my purse and briefcase on my shoulder as Kara and I walk out to the dining room where Eric, Blake, Adam, and Grayson wait. They all stand at our approach. "I'm headed to the building now," Adam says. "I just wanted to make sure you know I'm there. I wanted to make contact with you before you leave."

"Thank you," I say, and he nods and takes off for the door.

"Asher and one of our other men are in a surveillance van by the building," Blake says. "They'll be tapped into every camera in the building and any recording device Kara places will feed to them." He eyes Kara. "You need to go now."

She turns to me and her hands go to my shoulders. "Be you. Try to tune out what's going on. That's the best thing you can do. If you would normally get mad at him, get mad. Don't suddenly change with him. I'll be close."

"Thank you," I say.

"I want to be in the surveillance van," Grayson says.

"If you aren't at work today," Blake says, "that's going to be a red flag if he had her followed."

"If he had her followed, she'll be in trouble," Grayson says. "I need to be in that van."

"We came up with a story," I say. "You made me come visit you to get a payout on an investment. I'm angry about it. I'm team Ri."

Grayson's eyes narrow. He doesn't like this answer. He looks at Blake. "You better fucking protect her or I don't care how many skills you have. You will feel the pain."

"Grayson," I hiss. "Stop."

Blake looks at me. "If it were me with Kara I'd say the same thing." He looks at Grayson. "I'll protect her with my life."

"You better," he says, looking at me. "Because I don't have one without her. I can't lose her again."

It's then, in his intensity, that I know he knows something I don't know but there isn't time for me to ask. I have to get to the office and into the snake's den. I have to get to my meeting with Ri.

CHAPTER THIRTY-SIX

Grayson

The past, two years ago

I pull the Porsche to the front of the gallery where the annual children's hospital charity event is taking place with Mia in the seat next to me. "Oh my God, I'm nervous," she murmurs.

I grab her hand and kiss it. "You have no reason to be nervous."

"It's our first public outing," she argues. "And your father is going to be here. He wasn't supposed to be here."

The valets try to open the doors but I leave them locked, focused on Mia. "My father loves you."

"He and I had the coffee shop encounter. That's all. He went out of the country right after he talked to me that day. And he wasn't supposed to be here tonight," she repeats.

"You're here and on my arm. We're doing what he suggested. Owning our relationship. He was motivated to show up."

She turns to me. "The entire staff will know I'm fucking you."

I laugh. "Well since you're living with me, I think that, yes, they will assume that we're fucking."

"Are we really telling them I moved in with you?"

"Baby, we've been together six months and you haven't stayed at your place since. I'm in love with you, Mia. You're in love with me. It's time to stop hiding." The valet knocks on the window. "We need to get out. We're blocking the drive. I'll come around to get you." I hesitate. "Or we can leave. If you don't want—"

"No. I do. I don't want to hide. I'm established enough at work. I love you. Let's do this." She turns toward the door and I hit the locks. I step out of the car and hand the valet a large bill that shifts his scowl to a smile.

I round the vehicle and do the same for the guy on Mia's side and then I take her hand, walking her to me, and to the sidewalk just outside the door and behind a pillar. "You look beautiful," I say, giving her curves in a flesh tone, sparkling, knee-length gown a once over. "Get used to spending my money. It looks good on you."

"I don't have to. You do it for both of us. You had a dozen gowns delivered, Grayson. That's excessive."

"You wouldn't shop. I didn't know what you'd like, but for the record, this was the one I wanted you to wear."

"I don't ever want you to think I care about the money."

"You can't live life with me and keep fighting the money, baby. I have it. I damn sure don't want to spend it alone."

"I know, but—"

I lean in and kiss her. "We don't argue unless we're naked, remember?"

"You win all those arguments."

"That's the idea." I wink. "Come, baby." I slide her arm to my elbow. "Let's go donate some money to charity and tell the world we're in love."

She catches my arm. "Are you sure you love me enough to do this? Because I can't risk my career if you don't really love me."

"Where did that just come from?" I cup her face. "I love you like I didn't think I could love, but if you don't love me enough to—"

"I do. You know I do."

"Then we're going now. Stop thinking so much." I pull her under my arm, sheltering her with my body and making sure she knows how completely I'm claiming her.

We enter the gallery and we're greeted at the door by a hostess who directs us toward one of the event rooms. We travel the long walkway and I slide our fingers together right as Mitch, Mia's direct supervisor, walks out of the room we're about to enter. He stops dead in his tracks, looking stunned. "What is happening?"

"I asked to meet with you for the past three days," Mia says. "I wanted to warn you."

He looks at Grayson. "I—what does this mean?"

"It means we live together, we're in love, and Mia gets no special treatment."

"I don't want it," she says. "I think I've proven I'm good at my job. I'll continue to prove that I'm good at my job."

I fix him in a stare. "You can continue to be an asshole and ignore your employee's request for a meeting for three days if you like, though that's not a behavior I personally practice. I believe you've gotten a meeting with me immediately each time you've asked."

"I have," Mitch says glancing at me. "I'm sorry, Mia, and I'm not saying that because you're with Grayson. I was a shit to put you off." He looks at Grayson. "I'm having trouble with a case. I might need your counsel."

"Call me in the morning," I say.

Mitch nods and steps around us, "Oh my God," I whisper. "You just--"

"That had nothing to do with you, Mia," I say. "I don't approve. That's not how I operate. That's not how my father operates and he deserved to get sideswiped."

"Grayson, damn it."

I turn her to face me. "You're my woman. If he's a dick to you, he's a dick to other people. He doesn't get away with that. I expect you to tell me if there is anything that doesn't represent me the way you know I want to be represented. Earn your own way, I get that, but you're still my woman. We've talked about this. The only way to be my woman is to protect me and protecting my company is protecting me."

"I know that. You're right. We talked about this in advance."

"Okay then." I wrap my arm around her shoulder and kiss her temple. "Let's go in."

We enter the room with artwork on every wall, rows of small standing tables, and waiters maneuvering through the suits and tuxedos. We're only a few steps into the chaos, but I'm aware of all the eyes that turn in our direction as I'm certain Mia is as well. Thankfully a waiter stops in front of us, deflecting the attention sure to stir her discomfort. "Champagne?" he offers.

Mia holds up her hands but I accept two glasses. "You need this," I say, as the waiter departs.

"I might run my mouth and say who knows what if I drink this," she says, accepting the glass I hand her.

"If it makes you relax, that's a good trade-off." I hold my glass up to hers. "To us."

Her eyes warm. "To us," she says softly, the charge between us electric, the room fading away. My hand goes to her hip and I walk her closer. "We couldn't hide this, Mia. It's too damn good."

"Look who's here."

At the sound of the familiar voice, I grimace, releasing Mia to settle my hand at her back as we turn to face my old college rival. "Mia," I say, standing toe to toe with the man whose father has always been my father's business rival, his blond hair smoothed back ever so firm tonight, a silent standoff that I don't invite. He's just always fucking competing with me. "This is Riley Montgomery," I say. "You probably know him from the Montgomery firm. We went to school together."

"Call me Ri," Riley says, offering his hand to Mia and I swear I don't want to let her take it.

Mia does the expected and shakes his hand but when she would pull back he holds onto it. "You're lovely. When he's done with you, come see me. I'll help you lick your wounds."

Mia yanks her hand back. "That was inappropriate," she scolds before I can respond.

He chuckles. "I'm just an inappropriate guy."

"Try bitter. He wanted the girl who wanted me in college. I fucked her. He didn't." I look at Mia. "Just so he doesn't get the chance to tell the story and twist it on his own."

"Oh," Mia says, looking at Ri. "I'm sorry. That must have sucked."

Ri's scowl is instant. "You're sorry? You will be when he fucks you and moves on."

It's in that moment that my father joins us, stepping between Mia and Ri. "Mia, honey," he says, taking her hand. "I'm so glad to see you here and on Grayson's arm. You look stunning despite your present company." He glances at Ri. "How's your pops?"

"Opening four new offices in the next four months."

"Is he now?" he replies. "Better be careful. Too many too fast can cause grave growing pains. Good luck though."

He glances at Mia. "Walk with me and talk." He settles her hand on his elbow and turns her away from me and Ri.

Ri steps closer. "Obviously your father thought you needed help."

"I'm fairly certain my father wanted to flirt with Mia, just like you tried to flirt with Mia."

He narrows his eyes on me. "You're really into her." His lips twitch. "Interesting. In this case, I'll take your sloppy seconds. Let me know when you're done." He turns and walks away and for the first time ever, Ri hits a nerve.

Mia

"He's an absolute ass," Grayson's father says, guiding me through the crowd and down a corridor where more art is displayed. "But he came by it honestly. His father is as well. He and I went to law school together and the rivalry started there."

"That's a long time to be rivals," I say. "And are you really even rivals? You're about double their size, right?"

"Thanks to Grayson, who's a believer in thinking outside the box." He stops us at a painting of a winery. "Ever been to Sonoma?"

"A few weeks ago with Grayson. It was my first time."

"And you enjoyed it?"

"It was lovely." I laugh. "I liked all the cheap wines. I guess I'm a Brooklyn girl with Brooklyn taste buds."

He laughs. "And what did Grayson think of your choices?"

"He liked them. We brought some back with us."

"*Us.* Interesting choice of words. Do you still love my son?"

I nod. "Yes, Mr. Bennett. Very much." And I don't know why but I tear up.

He reaches up and wipes away the dampness. "First. Call me Raymond. Second, why did that make you cry? Does he not love you?"

"I just—I don't know how to deal with your money. I feel like when I tell you that I love him, you'll think I love the money. I feel like when I tell him I love him, he will on some level always wonder. I mean tonight he had twelve dresses delivered because I wouldn't shop. He wants me to spend his money, but I can't." I down my champagne and set the glass on a table. "I'm telling you this for a reason because you are the only person I know who can help me."

"How is it that I can help?"

"You said your wife hated the money, so she didn't want money when she met you."

"No, she did not."

"Did you doubt her? Did you ever think she wanted the money and not you?"

"Never. Not once, but she had to get over the fear of my money, as do you, of Grayson's. If you love him you have to share his life, and who he is, and money is a part of who he is, like it or not."

"If I spend his money, how does he know it's not about the money, because it's not. God, it's so not. I do love your son."

"Because I know," Grayson steps to my side and turns me to face him. "I know," he repeats. "If I didn't know, I wouldn't be so damn in love with you." He pulls me to him and kisses me. "I'm not letting you go. Don't you let me go."

"Never," I promise.

"Well then," his father says. "Sounds like we need to plan a family day in the Hamptons."

A family day, I think. Are these two men now my family? We start strolling the corridor, and as we laugh and talk, the clear moral compass of father and son, echo within each other, stirring admiration in me. I decide, that yes, I'd like very much to call them family and I have this sudden realization that I'm not so alone anymore. I tighten my grip on Grayson's arm and when he automatically covers my hand with his, I decide he's a part of me now. I not only won't let go of him, I can't.

CHAPTER THIRTY-SEVEN

Mia

The present

The room is silent for several beats after Grayson's guttural declaration from the other side of the dining room table that he can't live without me. Everyone stares at us. He stares at me. I stare at him. I just want to run into his arms and tell everyone to leave and that's what he wants, too, but that's not possible. That's not what can happen. We have to end this. He's only letting me do this to ensure Ri can't come between us again through this crazy plot to take him down.

"What now?" I force myself to ask, looking around the room.

"I for one," Kara states, "have to go." She starts walking backward. "See you soon, Mia!" she calls out and then rotates and hurries away.

Blake reaches in a bag and pulls out a blonde wig as well as a scarf. "These are for you, Mia." He closes the space between us and hands it to me. "I'll follow you out of the building and onto the subway. I'll be with you the entire time. Once you're in the tunnel, find a bathroom and dump the wig." He glances at his watch. "Do it now."

I nod and hurry to the bathroom off the foyer, pull on the wig and scarf, and barely look at the stranger in the mirror. I just want out of here. I want to get this meeting with Ri behind me and know if I've kept him oblivious to us being onto him. The minute I step back into the foyer, Blake hands me a lightweight unlined trench coat. "Put it on to hide your clothes and then dump it with the wig. Now, back to you exiting this building. Walk out like you belong here, not like you don't want to be seen."

"Got it," I say, mentally comparing it to the first day of court. You're nervous but you fake confidence until you feel it.

Grayson joins us in the foyer and steps to Blake's side, but it's me that's on his mind, me he's focused on, though he doesn't comment on the wig and like me, I think he barely notices. We both have too much else on our minds to care about my fake hair. Instead, he pulls me to him. "Remember what I told you. Just contain Ri and then do your job. Focus on your client and let us focus on Ri."

"I will," I say, my hand resting on his chest, his heart thundering beneath my palm, telling me how worried he is right now, which is why I add, "I promise."

He kisses me, a deep, drugging kiss, and then with obvious reluctance, he releases me "Let me just do this," I say, to both of them. "I go to this job every day. This is not going to be a big deal."

Eric steps into the foyer and gives me a nod, admiration and friendship in his eyes. We both love Grayson and in that there is a bond several years strong, a bond of understanding. He knows I have to protect Grayson and while I plan to keep my promise to Grayson, Eric knows me well enough to know that I'd sacrifice myself for the man I love. I turn away from Eric and I can't seem to look at Grayson again and actually walk out of the door. Right now he and I are making each other crazy and I just have to push forward and leave.

I exit the apartment into the hallway and Blake is quick to step to my side. "I'm riding down with you," he says, "but don't acknowledge me once we're in the car. There are cameras. I'll exit after you when we reach the lobby. I'll be with you all the way to the building even if you think I'm not there."

"What don't I know?" I ask, focused on my man, not myself. "Somehow Grayson is more on edge than he was before you arrived, and yet, he's letting me go to work."

"He needed to know that I take your safety seriously," Blake says. "I told him a personal story that shook him. One I'm not telling you now, but I'll summarize. He trusts me now. You can, too."

We round the corner and I punch the elevator button. "Grayson doesn't get rattled," I say. "What the heck kind of story was it?"

"A necessary one," he says. "And from my read on Grayson, he doesn't get rattled unless it's over you, which could be said of me with Kara."

The elevator opens and my chance to find out more does as well. We step inside and it begins; the day I pretend to be oblivious to all of Ri's bad deeds even as they work to destroy the man I love. The idea that I may have helped him by distracting Grayson grinds through me and by the time I exit the elevator and head for the exit, that's all I can think about.

The walk to the subway is short. I enter and hurry to the bathroom, and because it's busy, I dump my wig and coat in a bathroom stall, because that's the only way I won't be seen doing it. Once I leave my disguise behind, I rush out of the bathroom and toward the stairs leading to my train. I don't see Blake again, but I can feel his energy nearby, which is far more comforting than I realized it would be considering this is my normal route to work. It's safe, or rather it always felt as safe as you can be in New York City.

The ride is short and crowded. Once the train arrives at my stop, I exit the car, and then the tunnel, and check my watch. I have just enough time to make my normal coffee run and get to my desk and "normal" seems like a smart move today. I'm just paying for my coffee when I wonder how Blake dealt with anyone following me from my apartment, but I assume they have a plan. The fake me probably changed clothes and hair like I just did.

With my white mocha in hand, I finish my short walk to work, enter the corporate offices for the Montgomery firm and wave to the security guard Josh, as I always do. All normal things. This is a normal day, I tell myself. Just be normal. The lecture doesn't work. Nerves assail me but I refocus on this day being just like any other. As Grayson pointed out, I have a client who needs me. I'll use my energy to process her case. I step onto the elevator and end up chatting with a co-worker which while awkward at first, helps me settle into a calmer spot.

Soon, I'm inside the main offices, walking toward my own when I spy Kara. She's at a desk in the cubicle area, not far from my office, and talking to my supervisor, Kevin Murphy. All is well. I'm safe. Grayson will know that I'm safe. Ri could come at me here and never get to touch me though I doubt he'd come at me. I mean, why would he?

I enter my office, put my things away and my phone buzzes immediately. "Mia?"

At the sound of Ri's secretary's voice, my lips tighten. I punch the button on my speaker. "Yes, Tabitha?"

"Ri's confirming that you're on your way to his office?"

I curl my fingers into my palm. "I am," I say, and releasing the button, I grab my phone, stuff it in my skirt pocket and then round my desk to walk toward my door.

I'm about to exit when my boss steps in my path. "How's your case looking? I know you're passionate about this one."

Kevin's a tall, dark, and good-looking guy that might be a hottie to some, but for me, he has always had this big brother quality that feels safe and friendly. He cares about people. He loves the legal system. He's the one who's made it possible for me to pretend I don't work for Ri. "It's shaping up well," I say, "but I have to be in Ri's office now. Tabitha just called my desk to make sure I'm on the way."

"Again," he states with obvious disapproval.

"Yes. Again. You should know that he found out that I am looking for a job."

He blanches. "A job? Mia, why? You're successful here. Is it money? Do I need to fight for a raise?"

"No," I say, "but thank you. It's personal."

"It's because of Ri," he says, and it's not a question. "He's always coming at you. I knew that was going to get old for you."

"It's complicated. I'll update you on my status after I talk to him but thank you for caring."

"Caring and doing something to help are two different things. I can't help you with Ri but I wish I could. I'll try though. Let me know and I'll try." Words that could cost him his job and I won't let that happen. I do, however, let him walk away. He's better off staying away, too.

I watch him depart and Kara glances in my direction but doesn't acknowledge me. I cut down the hallway, turn a corner, and then enter Ri's private space through glass doors that lead me directly to Tabitha's desk. "He's waiting on you," she says, shoving her long red hair from her beautiful blue eyes. She's pretty, and I've often thought her to be involved with Ri, and yet he keeps coming at me, but then, really he's coming at Grayson through me.

I nod and walk around her desk and stop at Ri's door where I knock. "Come in!" he shouts.

I mentally steel myself for this encounter and enter to find him standing with his back to me at the window to the right of his massive black oval desk. "Shut the door," he says without turning.

Shut the door.

I do not want to shut the door and yet it's not an unreasonable request. I have to shut the door.

I shut the door and just like that, I'm alone with Ri. No, I'm alone with the devil himself.

CHAPTER THIRTY-EIGHT

Mia

Ri turns to face me the minute the door shuts, running a hand through his blond sleek hair. "Really, Mia? I helped you in a time of need and you're looking for a job?"

That sets me off and I forget fear. "*Helped me*? Are you serious? What happened to you're a fine attorney and we want to win the bidding war? What happened to me being a damn good attorney?" I walk further into the room, stopping in front of his desk between the two visitor's chairs but facing him at the window. "It was never about me now, was it? It was about fucking Grayson by fucking his woman if you could make it happen."

"His woman?"

"Oh my God, Ri. Stop. I'm talking past tense. You wanted to fuck me to fuck him and now that you know you can't, you act like a total asshole to me. You throw files on my desk. You demand updates on my cases. I don't even report directly to you. I can't believe I was this stupid." I rotate and start to walk away.

He closes the space between us and grabs my arm, whirling me around. "That's not how it is."

"Let go of me, Ri, or I swear the next knee I give you will do permanent damage and right now, I think it would be a good thing to prevent you from ever producing a mini-me."

"Did you really just say that to me?"

"Let go of me Ri. You have about thirty seconds or I *will* knee you and scream."

His jaw clenches. "Fuck, Mia." He releases me. "Happy?"

"No," I say. "I cannot be happy in the middle of this war. That's the problem but I have a client I really care about that I want to help. If you can't let me do my job then at least let me bring another attorney that I pick up to speed. You owe me that for using me like you have."

"I didn't use you. I want you. I want to be what he couldn't be for you and you know that. That's why you agreed to go out with me."

"I went to dinner with you because—it was a bad night. It was—I'd seen—"

"Grayson all over the papers with another woman. I know. I thought finally you saw the truth. He was always a ladies' man. Always, Mia. He fucked my woman in college. He fucked everyone's woman and yet, you said his fucking name in my home. You can't get over him."

"Maybe I never will," I say. "My heart is still with him. I can't change that, and you can't change it because you're like his stalker ex-girlfriend. All you care about is hurting him. You never wanted me."

His cellphone rings and he ignores it. "Stalker ex-girlfriend? Holy fuck, Mia. Did you write out that insult before coming in here?"

"You're obsessed to the point of it being scary. I don't want to be in the middle of this. Part of me wants to move to another city. I just want out."

"If I proved you wrong about Grayson—if I made you see that *you* matter, not him? Then what?"

"My God, Ri. What would happen if you did fuck me? Would you take out an announcement in *The New York Times* to make sure Grayson knew? Stop trying to fuck me already and if you can't, then let me out of my contract. Be a decent person and let me go."

He scrubs his jaw and looks away before fixing me in a stare. "You're a damn good attorney. I won't let you out of your contract. I'll back off and hope that one day you see that I have a sincere interest."

"The day you stop going after Grayson, I won't even know who you are. Maybe introduce yourself then."

"I'm not going after Grayson."

"Maybe not actively, but we both know if you get the chance, you'll take it. I don't want to be a part of that, Ri. Am I staying or are you letting me go?"

The phone on his desk buzzes and Tabitha speaks over the intercom. "Someone named RJ says it's urgent. He's on line two. Do you want it?"

Ri positively scowls. "Yeah. I want it." He looks at me. "Don't move." He stalks to his phone, grabs it, and picks up the line. "I told you not to call me at the office. I fucking meant it. I'll call you back." He hangs up and looks at me. "You have a contract, Mia. I'm not letting you out of it." His jaw sets hard. "Go back to work."

I get the sense he suddenly wants me out of his office and that it's connected to that call. I don't fight his demand. I don't have to. He doesn't know about me and Grayson. I'd know. He's just pissed at me, but he won't let me go. Not when I'm a weapon against Grayson. I open the door to exit and instinct has me turning to face his office before I push his door shut, and just in time to see him reach in his left draw and pull out a phone and it's not the one that was normally in his pocket.

I quickly shut the door and I don't look at Tabitha. I walk past her and to my office that I enter and shut the door. The minute I'm inside, I pull my phone from my pocket and send a group text: *Someone named RJ called the office phone and Ri got pissed. He told him not to call him here. When I was leaving he didn't know I turned around and saw him open his left drawer and pull out a phone and it wasn't the one he normally had in his pocket. I think it was a burner phone and I think he was calling that RJ person.*

Blake answers immediately: *We'll get the number off the phone and tap it.*

But how? I think. Surely Ri will take that phone home tonight. I'm shocked he kept it in his desk at all but he must have a reason.

My phone buzzes again with another message from Blake: *You did good, Mia. FYI we haven't swept your office yet. Don't hold conversations that could be damaging.*

I inhale and fight the urge to call Grayson. That's what he was telling me. Don't call Grayson and Grayson can't call me or text me. He's silent and I wonder if he was listening. I wonder if there was something I said that he didn't like and it's killing me. I can't take it. I dial his number. "Mia," he breathes out into the phone.

"Did you—"

"Every word."

"You didn't—"

"You don't want in the middle of this war. I heard you. You said that to me, too."

"I was hurt and angry when I said that to you."

"You were telling the truth," he replies. "And I don't want you in the middle of it and yet, there you are today, right in the middle."

"That's not your fault."

"Yes. It is. I didn't end this a year ago when he sent Becky to my office to fuck us the way he wants to fuck you. That's right. Asher found electronic proof that Mitch and Becky were working for Ri. We no longer have to speculate. You won't be in the middle long, Mia. Of that, you can be certain."

"What does that mean?"

"A conversation better had in person."

My stomach knots. "You're not talking about us, right?"

"No, Mia, I am not talking about us. We do not end ever again. Stay out of his way today. And I'll make sure he stays out of your way from this point forward." My phone on my desk buzzes and he says, "I'll be close, baby." Grayson hangs up and the receptionist says, "Delaney Wittmore is on the line."

My client, who I need to talk to. "Put her through," I say, trying to shake off the idea that the worst thing that ever happened to Ri was for Grayson to hear that conversation which wouldn't bother me if I knew what that meant, but I don't. What is Grayson about to do and what consequences will that have for him and us? I need to see him. I need to talk to him, and yet, I cannot. I'm here, trapped inside a world that Ri controls.

I grab the phone. "Hi, Delaney."

"Mia, how are things coming along? Do we have a trial date? Is there any hope of ending this without one?"

"There's always hope." We talk a good fifteen minutes and we've just hung up when Kevin pops his head in the door.

"You're still on staff?"

"Yes," I confirm. "For now, all remains the same."

"Are you looking for a job?"

"Not anymore."

"Good. Then we have a team meeting at six. It's the only way to get past everyone's court schedule."

"Six. Yes. Okay. I'll be here."

He disappears and now I officially know that I'll be here late, after hours and exposed in a sparsely occupied office. I grab my phone and decide against a group text that might make it to Grayson and set him off. I text Kara instead: *I have to be here for a six pm staff meeting.*

She replies: *I know. I overheard Ri telling Kevin to set it up. He's behind the meeting. Stay alert and I'll stay close.*

I type, *I'll see you there and thank you, Kara,* and then set my phone down, letting this news sink in. Ri, who doesn't have any direct interaction with our team, set up this meeting. Ri wants me here late. He's up to something.

CHAPTER THIRTY-NINE

Grayson

I don't want to be in the middle of this war.

Mia's words stay with me for the hours that follow her shouting them at Ri. I don't know how the hell I manage to go to the office, but I do. I go. I work. I get frequent, and thankfully uneventful, updates, and come early evening, Eric takes over a problem I'm managing, and Blake picks me up in the parking garage to take me back to the surveillance van.

"Nothing new," he says when I join him in the backseat of an Escalade with one of his men in the front seat. A guy named Savage with a scar down his face who looks brutal enough for me to want to introduce him to Ri. "At least not where Mia's concerned. Ri's another story. I have a lot to share." He hands me a data drive. "Everything I'm about to tell you is backed up with proof on that drive."

I pocket it. "I'm listening."

"Ri's been in bed with Rosemond, the mob affiliate I told you about since he left college. That's how he's won about every accomplishment he's had. If someone says no, he pays Rosemond and he breaks out the proverbial baseball bat. I can't prove it yet, but based on the cash withdrawals Ri is making that never show up anywhere else, I think he's being blackmailed, most likely by

239

Rosemond. That's how he works. He does your dirty work and turns it around on you."

"And you know what you know how?"

"Data doesn't go away. When you think you've wiped it, it's not gone. The right person, and that's me, can find it. I did. Give me time, which Mia created today, and I'll put all the pieces together. Right now though, there's heat on you. You have to make a decision. Use what I found to back him off and create a standoff, or wait and risk the DA coming at you before we act."

"He's already involved the DA. Davis has a source that confirmed that with details of pending charges."

"And I have a source that confirmed that to be true but it's not where I can get to it. Not yet."

"Then we don't know what bullshit Ri gave them already and Ri can't just pull back from the DA and say he was joking to save his ass. We have to prove that I'm innocent."

"Agreed," Blake says, "but you could stop him from delivering any further blows by going at him."

"We could also shove the traitors in my operation into a hole and we won't find them until they're in trouble again."

"But we stop them and Ri from handing over damning information to the DA or planting fake information the DA finds in a raid. Right now, there is nothing in the DA's system on you."

"Per an insider at the DA's office, I assume?"

"Per their computer system that I hacked."

I arch a brow. "You hacked the DA?"

"Yes, I've also worked for the DA and hacked for the DA." He moves on. "Look, here's my concern. Rosemond. He's my concern. If he's blackmailing Ri, Ri could be trying to connect him to you and get rid of both of you at once. If he's not trying to get rid of Rosemond and you take down

Ri, as I've said, you've hurt his money and you become a target."

"Mia becomes a target."

"Exactly. Mia and your company, because those things are what matter to you, in different ways, of course. We need to turn Rosemond on Ri, and get Ri focused on protecting himself from Rosemond."

"Which he could do by turning the heat on him and me with the DA. That doesn't work."

"It works if we have the proof we need to prove he set you up first."

His phone rings and he pulls it from his pocket. "Sorry, man. This is one of my men on assignment overseas. I have to take it."

I nod and he answers his call. My mind goes to my father and I try to think about what he'd do right now, even what advice he'd give me which transports me back to the last piece of advice he ever gave me. Back to the day he died and that golf course in the Hamptons:

"You're shooting like hell, son. I'd ask why but we both know why. You haven't been good since she left. You damn sure haven't been able to be here, in the Hampton's since she left."

"I've made more money for me and the company in the past six months than I have in my entire career."

"I don't give a flip about the money," he says, turning to face me, his hands settling on his hips. *"I care about you and her. She loves you. You love her. Go get her."*

"She's with Ri now."

"She's working for Ri. There's a difference between fucking him and working for him."

"Oh come on, pops. She thinks I fucked Becky. She's fucking Ri."

"Have you asked her?"

"She won't even talk to me." I pull the ring out of my pocket, where I've held it every day for six months. "She sent it back."

"Well, you damn sure know she didn't want your money."

"I already knew that."

He throws his golf bag in the rear of the cart and I do the same. "Make her listen."

"Becky was naked and pressed against me, dad. No words erase that."

He turns away from me and presses a hand on the rear of the cart. "Fuck." He fists his hand on his chest. "I don't—feel right, son."

"What? What does that mean?"

"I don't know. I can't seem to breathe. Call—"

He falls to his knees and I go down with him. "Dad. Fuck." I dial 911 and then it's like a tunnel consumes me. I have random moments of clarity. Me pumping my father's chest. Me shouting for help. The emergency crew. The ambulance and me riding beside my father, holding his hand. And then his final words, "Son, protect what was mine and what is yours. Do not let anyone take what is yours. Don't let anyone take who you love."

And then he'd shut his eyes and never opened them again.

"Sorry about that," Blake says, drawing me back to the present. "But, fuck. My man is in some heat right now, but then so are you. The most important thing right now is proving you're innocent. Once we get that proof, and that could be a few keystrokes from happening, then we ensure Ri pays, and that Rosemond doesn't come at you."

"You turn them on each other," I supply since that's where we're going with this conversation.

"Yes. I can make Rosemond believe Ri is setting him up even if he's not. That gets Ri fighting for his life, not trying to take yours. I'll then have a friend at the FBI offer him protection to turn evidence on Rosemond. That means Ri is out of the picture and in witness protection. But there are risks. Ri could end up dead and I need to know you know that. I'll do my best to ensure that doesn't happen. This protects you and Mia. That's my priority."

Ri could end up dead.

This protects Mia.

My father's words come back to me: *Son, protect what was mine and what is yours. Do not let anyone take what is yours. Don't let anyone take who you love.*

"Do it," I say and I feel no remorse. Mia is my first priority. My company and my employees are my second priority. Ri is nothing and I do believe that even my father, with his strict moral compass, would want him to know it.

Blake pulls us up to the high-rise where Ri's offices are and into a parking garage. A few minutes later, I'm sitting in a surveillance van watching Mia on a camera as she joins a staff meeting. Ri enters the room and instead of looking around the room and communicating to the room of twenty, his gaze lands on Mia. He can't take his eyes off her and if I sit here, watching this much longer, Rosemond might not need to kill Ri. I will. For forty-five minutes, he lectures the team about production and projections that aren't where he wants them to be. For forty-five minutes, the entire room has to know he can't keep his eyes off fucking Mia. It's almost like he knows I'm watching.

The meeting ends and Mia, like the rest of the group, stands, only when she would escape, Ri calls out her name, "Mia, my office before you leave."

That's a mistake. He has no idea what a mistake he just made because if he touches her again, I'm not staying in this van.

CHAPTER FORTY

Mia

After ordering me to his office, Ri heads out of the conference room. My mind races and I know I'm headed into dangerous territory with him. I sense it. "Mia?" Kevin asks. "Do you need help?"

"No. Thanks. Goodnight." I rush toward the door and spy Ri already headed down the hallway. "Ri!"

He stops and turns. "My office."

"I'm running to the bathroom first," I say, needing an excuse to talk to Kara who is no longer at her desk but it's her I need. "I'll be there in three minutes."

"Make it two," he snaps, his jaw set hard, anger radiating off of him the way it had the entire meeting which was generally miserable, as he kept staring me down. In turn, Kevin scowled at him, and everyone knew it was about me.

I rush down the hallway to a bathroom nearby, step inside and enter the stall and since I don't know if this room is being recorded, I pull out my phone and text Kara: *I'm going to be in his office. Create a distraction. Get him out of there long enough for me to get the number off that phone in case he takes it home tonight. And yes, I know Grayson won't approve which is why I'm texting only you.*

Kara calls me and I answer. "You're safe to talk where you're at and no, Grayson won't approve, but you have to do it. I'll get him out of there and I'll warn you by phone when he's returning. The risk is minimal as the office is all but empty. Just get the number and get clear of the desk. Text it to us right away."

"Got it."

"Go. Now."

I hang up and I know I have to do this. I can't keep coming here. Grayson won't be able to take it. I feel it. I know it. I have to help where I can and be prepared not to come back. I stick my phone in my pocket and exit the bathroom. My path back to Ri's office is swift. Once I'm there I find Tabitha gone and the door open. I step inside. "Shut the door," he orders from behind his desk where he stands leaning on the hard surface.

"No one is out there."

"Shut the fucking door, Mia."

I remind myself that I'm wearing a wire. I have plenty of help nearby. I shut the door and lean against it. "Afraid?" he asks.

"You're acting weird."

"I know you were with Grayson this weekend."

I'm stunned despite being prepared and I react instantly. "You had me followed? Really, Ri? I've been here a year. Have you had me followed the entire time?"

"He's a competitor. It's reasonable."

"That's a yes. I can't believe you."

"*You were at his house.*"

"I don't have to explain myself, but yes, I was. He owed me money on an investment and he made me collect in person."

"For the entire weekend?"

"Yes, Ri. And now I know he and I are really over. I had to find out. I had to know."

"He fucked Becky. That was pretty over, or I thought it was. Maybe you don't give a shit what pussy he sticks his cock into as long as you have his money."

"You're a son of a bitch, Ri. I can't believe I ever came to work for you."

"Well you did, and you have a contract, and if you leave or betray me with him I'll destroy you."

His cellphone rings and my heart lurches with the hope that this is the distraction. He answers the line and scowls. "Towed? What the fuck? Stop them. Yes. I'll be right there." He rounds his desk. "My car is being towed. Do not fucking leave my office, Mia. You wait because we aren't done." He exits his office and I follow him, watching as he disappears through the glass doors.

Adrenaline shoots through me and I shut the door, rush to his desk and pull open the drawer, relieved to find the phone. I grab it, find the number, and text it to the group. I set it back in the drawer and quickly start searching drawers. I reach for the one beneath the phone and it's locked. I open his top desk drawer and find a key. Luckily it works which makes locking the drawer a joke, but thankfully Ri is funny like that.

I open the drawer and find a file that reads "Bennett" on it. I open it and want to be sick. It's all the records of the set-up, including a list of Grayson's employees being paid to help Ri. I shoot photos, lots of photos and decide I just need to take the file. This is all we need to end this. I text what photos I took to the group, shut the drawer, lock it and decide, that's it—I'm leaving. I rush out of his office and into mine because I need to seem normal. I need to seem like I just left mad, or quit. Otherwise, Ri will search his office. I grab my briefcase and computer, stick the file inside, and head for the elevator.

Still no warning about Ri which means he could come up the elevator at any moment. I don't know what areas of the office Kara can see. She might not even know where I'm standing. She might only be able to see Ri right now. I cut right and enter the stairwell, starting to run down the steps. It's a long way down but I just want out of here. I want out of this building and this office. Relief washes over me as I near the exit and I've just stepped off the final step when the door bursts open with Ri entering the stairwell.

My heart lurches. "I thought you forgot me. I was coming to make sure you were still here."

He glances at my briefcase and me and then growls, "Bullshit. You thought I'd take the elevator. And I just realized I left you in my office after you spent the weekend with Grayson."

He lunges for me and I turn to try to run but it's too little too late. He grabs my hair and all but rips it out as he yanks me around to face him. "What do you have in your bag?" He reaches for it, and I punch him, giving help time to arrive, I hope, but it does no good.

He reaches in my bag that I stupidly didn't zip and grabs the folder. "You little bitch." He drops it on the ground and shoves me against the wall. "I should have known you were still fucking him. That will never get out of this building."

"It doesn't matter. I took pictures. I sent proof to the police. Did you really think you could frame Grayson and get away with it?"

"I'll get away with it. You'll be dead and I'll tell them you were setting me up."

"Dead? You're going to kill me? Are you serious?"

"Yes, Mia. You'll die." He reaches in his pocket and pulls out his phone. "Mia will need to be dealt with tonight but not until I'm done with her. Pick her up at the normal spot." He ends the call. "We fuck first. Maybe you can talk me out of killing you."

I try to knee him but he catches my leg. "Not this time, sweetheart. This time I fuck you, you don't fuck me." He reaches in his pocket and pulls out a gun. "Just in case you think you might scream. Think again." He yanks me off the wall and starts pulling me by the hair toward the door. That's when the door bursts open and Grayson appears holding a gun followed by Blake.

"Grayson," I breathe out, as the two men stand side by side, Blake directly in front of Ri, but it's Grayson Ri is looking at, his gun now pointed at him.

"Let her go, Ri, or I will shoot you," Grayson says, stepping closer. "And I'll enjoy it."

Ri holds the gun on him to my head. "We walk out together or she leaves dead. Decide."

CHAPTER FORTY-ONE

Grayson

I charge at Ri in the hopes that he'll turn his gun on me, but he doesn't. He holds steady and I stop in front of Mia, not about to block Blake's shot if he so chooses to shoot the bastard before I do. Right about now, he probably wants to shoot me for taking one of his guns, but I don't give a damn. The minute I heard Mia went down the stairs and Ri decided to take the stairs instead of the elevator, I wasn't waiting for her to end up dead.

"I'll kill you, Ri," I promise. Mia's hand goes to my waist as if she just needs to touch me. I want to comfort her. I want to pull her into my arms, but I don't dare look away from Ri.

His eyes narrow on mine and I have a really fucking bad feeling he's about to pull the trigger, just to spite me, just to finally hurt me. "I love you, Grayson," Mia whispers, because yes, she feels his readiness too, but that's not the right thing for him to hear right now.

Fuck it, I'm going to kill him. My finger twitches on the trigger but a shot rings out before I shoot. Ri jolts backward and blood splatters all over my face and Mia's. I grab Mia and pull her to me. "What happened?" she asks. "What happened?!"

"Easy, baby," I say, looking over her shoulder at Ri lying across the floor, with a bullet between his eyes and blood pooling around him, thick and wide.

Blake appears by my side and takes my gun, "Thank me later. He was going to shoot and I wasn't letting you answer for that. Get her out of here." He kneels beside Ri and checks for a pulse as Adam charges in the door, "Get me an ambulance and the police," Blake shouts at him.

I cup Mia's face and tilt her eyes to mine. "You're okay?"

"He's dead, right?"

"No pulse!" Blake shouts before I can answer. "Hurry the fuck up, Adam!"

"I called. They're on the way." Adam eyes me. "Get her out of here." He opens the door as I scoop up Mia and carry her past Adam, into the garage, and then to the van where I set her on the edge of the interior.

Sirens sound in the distance and Kara runs to our side. "Is she okay?" she asks and then to Mia. "Are you okay?"

"I'm alive," Mia says, burying her head in my stomach and clinging to my waist. I cradle her head, my gaze finding Kara's. "She's shaken. Give us a few." Kara nods and hurries away while I tilt Mia's face and ease her stare to mine. "You're okay, baby. I got you. You know that, right?"

"You could have been killed. I caused this. I didn't listen to you. He knew about us and I felt like it was now or never."

"I heard everything. You were right to just get out and while I'd have preferred you never see him again, you got him to admit everything on the audio. You did good."

"He's *dead*." Her voice cracks. "I didn't do good. *He's dead*."

"You did what he forced you to do and you tried to get out of his path." Sirens grow louder, now in the garage, closing in on us. "He was armed, Mia. Had we not called him to the garage what happened in the stairwell might have happened in his office and we might not have gotten to you in time."

The ambulance pulls up just behind us, followed by at least one police car, and Mia grabs my shirt in reaction. "Oh God. The world knows now. The news will be blasting everywhere. My father is going to find out. Call him, please. I can't talk to him. I'll cry and he'll freak out."

I pull my phone from my pocket and kneel beside her, punching in her father's autodial that I never deleted. "Mac," I say. "It's Grayson."

"Grayson? How the hell are you?"

"Listen, sir. Mia is with me and safe, but there's been an incident at her office. She's shaken but unharmed."

"What incident? I need to talk to her. Tell her I need to talk to her."

"Sir—"

"Grayson, damn it."

I cover the phone and look at Mia. "Baby. He needs to hear your voice."

She nods and takes the phone. "Hey, dad. Yes. No. My boss. He's crazy or he was. He's dead. No. I'm fine. Just— meet us at the apartment." She looks at me. "Grayson's apartment that's my apartment again. I hadn't had time to tell you."

"He's still on the security list," I say. "I'll have the building let him in."

She repeats my words and then hangs up right as Blake reappears. "The police are going to want to talk to you both. Just tell the truth." He looks at Mia. "You okay?"

"No, I'm not, but thank you. Grayson would have shot him, and I know what you did in that stairwell not only saved him trouble but you saved my life, Blake."

"I'm just glad I pulled the trigger before Grayson, who clearly knows how to handle a gun a little too well for my sanity today."

"My father insisted that a man with money had to know how to protect himself," I say. "And so, I do but thank you. I know you saved me a lot of grief. I would have killed him."

"It was justified," Blake says. "He was going to shoot, but it's less complicated this way."

"Then he really is dead?" Mia asks.

"He didn't have much of a chance," Blake replies. "I was taught to shoot to kill and I do. I wasn't giving him a chance to lift his gun and shoot because he would have." He eyes me. "I called Eric. He has an attorney on the way to represent you, though I see no reason this becomes a problem for you. In fact, thanks to Mia, tonight ends this for you both."

A police officer appears next to Blake, followed by a plainclothes detective, as does a tall man, in a blue suit, with a salt and pepper beard; Ridell Murphy, a ten-year veteran with the firm, and one of our best criminal defense attorneys. "Eric sent me," he says, which doesn't surprise me, as Eric respects the hell out of Ridell.

"Glad to have you with us, Ridell," I say.

"Yes," Mia agrees. "Good to see you right about now."

"I'd rather see you under different circumstances, Mia," Ridell says, and he's too much of a pro to ask how she is doing. He knows the answer: not well. Instead he and Blake take control of the questioning that comes at us hard and fast, and stretches for hours in one shape or another.

Blake repeats the same words over and over. "In my professional opinion Mia would be dead if I wouldn't have pulled that trigger when I did. We have cameras and audio for you to make your own assessments." He handles just about everything thrown our way before we can and owns it as his.

Once the police finish with us, Mia is shaking so hard that the EMS tech still on scene insists he check her out, quickly directing us to the bed inside the vehicle. I help Mia inside and when I would stay outside, and give the tech room to evaluate Mia, she isn't having it.

She pats the bed next to her and whispers, "Please."

I glance at the EMS tech, a fit, fifty-something man with gray hair, and he nods his approval.

I join Mia and sit next to her. "Joe" introduces himself and kneels next to Mia to check her vitals. "Shock," he declares after a short exam. "You really need something to calm your nerves."

"What I need is to go home," she says, looking at me. "Can we go home now?"

I reach up and brush her cheek. "Yeah, baby. We can go home." I glance at Joe. "Is she safe to go home?"

"She is, but if she doesn't stop shaking, you need to get her something to calm her nerves."

"I will," I assure him. "I have a doctor we can call if necessary."

Joe approves, and I exit the vehicle and help Mia down. Kara and Blake are waiting on us outside and an SUV pulls up next to them. Blake pats it. "Your ride. My man, Smith is behind the wheel. He'll take you home."

Kara hands Mia a sweater. "This will warm you up and cover up any mess."

"You mean blood," Mia says. "Thank you. My father is waiting on us at the apartment. I don't want to freak him out any more than he's probably freaked out already."

She hands Mia some sort of towelettes. "Clean your face in the car."

Mia touches her face. "I wiped it off earlier. There's more blood?"

"Yeah, honey, just a little bit," Kara says and looks at me. "You, too. You have a few lingering smudges."

I nod and then Blake and I shake hands while Mia and Kara hug. "I'm here if you need me," Kara promises Mia, pulling back to look at her. "That includes to talk. That was a rough scene back there and you're going to question yourself but don't. I guided you through what to do. You asked me. You didn't act alone. Furthermore, you were trying to just get out of there. That was a good thing."

"Agreed," Blake says, and then backing up what I already expressed he adds, "He had a gun. He knew about you and Grayson. I don't want to think about you waiting for him in his office, and us not getting to you in time."

"Where do we stand on backlash from Ri's cronies?"

"That file Mia grabbed assures you have none," he says. "It proved Ri was not only trying to frame you but Rosemond also."

"Who's Rosemond?" Mia asks.

"The mob affiliate Ri was involved with," Blake explains. "Ri was his gravy train and we didn't want Rosemond lashing out at you two for hurting his bottom line. That's how those types work. Thanks to you, Mia, he won't. We scanned the data from that file which involved him and sent it to him before I handed it over to the police. He now knows that Ri was trying to take him down. You're both free and clear. Go home. Rest. I'll be around if you have questions tomorrow."

We say our goodbyes and Mia and I climb in the backseat of the SUV and I pull her close. The minute we're moving, I cup her face and lean in, kissing her with a long stroke of my tongue, emotions I've suppressed for hours, all but bleeding from me into her. "I almost lost you tonight," I whisper, pressing my cheek to hers, my lip at her ear, "I would not have survived losing you." I pull back to look at her. "I can't lose you." I press my head to hers. "I would not have let him hurt you. No one will ever come that close again. You have my word."

She pulls back, too. "You told me to get in and get out. You're not mad at me?"

"You were trying. He wouldn't let you and you were protecting me." I stroke her hair from her face. "Most importantly, you're alive, so no, I'm not mad at you." I lean in and press my lips to her ear again. "But I might need to keep you in the bed, naked, and in my arms for a few days, just to convince myself you're really okay." I stroke her hair from her face. "And to make sure you know I have you. I'm not letting go. Ever, Mia."

"Promise?"

"Promise, baby," I say, pulling her into my arms and holding onto her. She lays against my chest, and she's still trembling, quaking inside and I just want to take away the fear and trauma. The only way I know to do that is just to hold her and keep holding her for the rest of our lives. And I will, but I'll do so just a little tighter right now until she's ready for me to loosen that hold. Until she heals.

CHAPTER FORTY-TWO

Grayson

On the ride to our apartment, we meet Smith, our driver and one of Blake's men, while Mia and I clean up as much of the blood we're wearing as possible. The clean-up is successful with the exception of my white shirt splattered with blood and there's no hiding it. "My father is going to freak out when he sees the blood," Mia worries. "What was I thinking having him come here?"

I stroke her hair. "You were thinking that he's going to hear all of this on the news if he doesn't hear it from you first. You did the right thing."

"Right," she says. "I'm glad one of us remembers what I was thinking."

"We're here," Smith announces, pulling us to the front of our building and I toss all the wipes we used in a trash bag at the back of his seat. "We'll have men here at your building indefinitely," he adds glancing back at us. "Just in case you have trouble with the press. I can also drive your father home Ms. Cavanaugh."

"Thank you," Mia says. "And call me Mia. I doubt he'll leave once he finds out what happened."

"I'll text you my number in case," Smith says. "I'll be here all night." He glances at me. "Would you like an escort to your door, sir?"

"A bodyguard will only freak out Mia's father," I say, "so unless you think we need one, we'll pass."

"Not until the press finds you," he says. "And right now, they're focused on the crime scene. You should be fine tonight."

I open the door. "Thank you, Smith."

"Yes, thank you," Mia says, and I'm encouraged by how much stronger she sounds, right up until the moment I help her out of the SUV and her knees give out.

She collapses against me and I hold onto her, the way I plan to hold onto her forever. "I got you, baby."

"I know you do," she says. "I know you do, and I can't believe I forgot that. You charged at him." Her voice cracks. "You tried to get him to point the gun at you. You knew he might shoot you."

"We protect each other, remember?"

"Don't *ever* risk your life like that again," she scolds, her voice suddenly strong, a crackle of anger beneath the surface. "Every time I think of you running at him, of what might have happened, I start to shake all over again."

I don't promise her I won't risk my life for her, because I would, I will, and I'd do it all over again to protect her. Instead, I maneuver her around me and shut the SUV door before setting us in motion toward the entrance to our building. The doorman, an older gentleman with white hair, is a new guy I don't know well. His eyes rocket to my shirt like it's a damn magnet, but he'll most likely assume I was in a fight, which isn't inaccurate. I stop and talk to him. "The press will be all over us in the morning. Be prepared."

"The press, sir?"

"Yes. The press. Don't say I didn't warn you." I urge Mia into the rotating doors, my hands on her hips, and I move with her, keeping her close.

We exit on the other side and I pull her back under my arm, guiding us to the front desk where Devon, a familiar young guard who knows us both works tonight. "Did Mia's father sign-in?" I ask.

"He did," Devon confirms, ignoring my shirt. I liked Devon before. I like him more now. He eyes Mia. "Nice to have you back, Mia."

"Thank you, Devon," she says, and I turn her away from the desk, eager to get both of us out of the public eye.

Once we're in the elevator, Mia inspects the blood all over me. "Your shirt looks horrible." She presses her hands to her face.

I pull them away. "Your father just needs to know that you're okay. Put him up in the spare bedroom and we'll all rest better."

"You never minded when he stayed."

"I only cared when you left."

"Grayson," she breathes out.

He cups my face. "I'm right here, baby. I'm not going anywhere."

The elevator halts and I kiss her, maneuvering us into the hallway as I do, and I keep us moving toward our apartment. We're almost at our door and I'm about to stop and ask her a few questions about her father when she steps in front of me, her hands on my chest, and *damn, I missed her* is all I can think of in this moment. "He can't know that I went to work for Ri for that bonus that saved him from his debt," she says. "He'll blame himself for tonight and it's not his fault. I should never have left you and no matter what, I should have to come to you. I just—I really didn't want you to think I was just coming for your money."

"We need to talk about leaving all of this behind us, but I need to know what your father knows before we walk into the apartment."

"I never told him you cheated," I say. "I just—I didn't want him to think badly of you. I never gave him real details at all."

Because on some level I know she knew I'd never cheat on her. "Then everything is between us and we'll keep it that way. Ri hated me. He went at you because of me. That will be in the news. We can't hide that from him. We shouldn't try."

"What about us being back together?"

"What about it, Mia?" I don't give her time to reply. "We're back together."

"That's right," she says, grabbing my tie. "So, don't go trying to get killed and leave me, Grayson." She turns away and I pull her to me.

"I could say the same to you. I was terrified when Ri entered that stairwell."

"I wasn't going to go back. I knew we couldn't take it. I just wanted to get what I could and get back to you."

"And you are. We'll talk later, baby. We have a lot to say. I know I do."

The door behind us opens. "Mia!"

She rotates and runs to her father, throwing her arms around him. The two of them hug and I give them a moment before I join them. Mac catches a glimpse of me over Mia's shoulder and his eyes go wide. "What the hell?" he murmurs setting her aside to look at me. "What happened to you?"

"Let's go inside and talk," I suggest, motioning them both forward.

"Yes," he says. "Let's."

I follow them into the foyer and Mac turns, waiting on me. Mia quickly joins me, standing by my side. "Dad—"

"What the hell happened to you, Grayson?" He's a fit man, his hair streaked with gray, his green eyes intense. His worry for his daughter obvious.

"Let's sit," I suggest.

"No," Mac says. "I don't want to sit. I want answers. Both of you, talk."

"My boss hated Grayson. He—" Mia inhales. "He—"

"Tried to hurt Mia to hurt me," I supply. "I hired professional help to deal with him. One of those men shot and killed Ri tonight."

"Holy fuck. Shot and killed?" He looks at Mia. "Where were you when it happened? Because obviously, Grayson was close."

"He was—I—" She looks down. "Grayson was holding a gun to his head," she looks at her father, "because he was holding a gun to my head."

Mac blanches. "What? He was—what?" He looks at me. "Why did this happen?"

"He knew how much I loved Mia and he was jealous of my success and my relationship with her."

"You were broken up," he snaps. "Why are you even back together?"

That statement hits me wrong, almost as if he's blaming me for Ri's insanity or that he was secretly glad to get rid of me. I bite my tongue but Mia snaps, pushing away from me. "This isn't his fault. He didn't make Ri a lunatic. Ri plotted our break-up. He tried to force himself on me. He is probably behind all the trouble you had last year because he knew if he offered me a bonus to save you I'd take a job with him. And why are we even back together? Really, dad? *Really*? I *love* Grayson. I've been miserable without him and I know you know that. I don't need to hear you blame him tonight."

She rushes past him and he catches her arm, turning her to face him. "You took the job to pay off my debt?"

"Yes. I did. It was all one big set-up. Ri didn't go after me because I got back with Grayson. He went after me and Grayson last year when this all started."

Mac's hands go to Mia's shoulders. "I wasn't blaming Grayson. And right now, I'm thanking God he's back because I know he loves you."

"You said 'why are you even back together' or whatever you said," she snaps back. "I didn't like it. I'm certain Grayson didn't either."

"I know he's covered in blood because he was right there with you, willing to risk his life to save you."

"He did risk his life to save me. He dared that man in every way to shoot him, not me, and Ri hated Grayson. I'm lucky he's alive. I'm really damn lucky he's alive. If I'd have lost him tonight, I'd be ready to go, too. Don't you see that?"

"I had a moment of freak out, Mia," Mac says. "It came out wrong. I love Grayson. I have always respected him and welcomed him to our family."

I step behind Mia, and settle my hands on her shoulders, silently offering her support.

"And as for my debt," Mac continues, "I hate that you went to that man for me. That means, this is my fault."

"No," Mia says. "It's not and I didn't want to tell you because I knew you'd say that. I let Ri turn me into a weapon against Grayson that is much deeper than you can imagine."

"I'm certain Grayson doesn't blame you." He kisses her forehead and turns to me. "I *am* glad that you're back. She was never happy without you." He offers me his hand which I accept. "You're a good man," he says. "Take care of my daughter."

"I will, sir, every day of the rest of her life."

He nods and turns to Mia. "I'm going to leave because as much as I want to stay, I sense that you and Grayson need time together. Come see me soon." He hugs her and looks at me. "Both of you." He looks at Mia. "I love you, daughter." He kisses her temple and then heads for the door.

The minute it shuts, I lock it and turn to Mia who is suddenly shaking all over again, adrenaline and emotions making for a bad cocktail when mixed with shock. I grab her, scoop her up and start carrying her toward our bedroom.

CHAPTER FORTY-THREE

Grayson

I set Mia on the white tiled ledge of the sunken tub and then walk to the shower, turning on the water. Once it's warming up, I walk back to her and stroke her cheek. "Stay right here," I order. "I don't want you to fall. You're still unsteady." I try to pull away but she catches my hand.

"Grayson."

"I'll be right back, baby. I want to get you something to take the edge off."

She nods and releases me and the fact that she welcomes whatever I bring her says a lot. Mia isn't a drinker and she hates drugs of any type. I walk out of the bathroom and into the bedroom, stopping at the mini-bar in one corner, pouring her a stout drink that she'll hate, but it'll help her relax.

I return to find her shoes kicked off and I go down on a knee beside her. "Drink," I order, pressing it into her hand and when her hand shakes on the way to her mouth, I help her hold onto the glass. "Like a shot. All at once."

She swallows hard and then downs the whiskey. "Oh God. That's horrible."

"That's a twenty-five-year-old scotch that cost ten thousand dollars a bottle."

"That's a lot of money for something that tastes that bad."

I laugh. "It's good stuff. Even better with the second glass."

"It made me warm all over."

"I'd rather it be me that makes you warm all over."

"Then take that damn bloody shirt off. I can't look at it."

"Let's both just strip down and I'll get rid of our clothes." I set the glass down, stand up and take her with me.

She fumbles with my buttons and I take over, quickly pulling it over my head and then walk to the trash can, hit the lever with my foot, and stuff the shirt inside. "Better?"

"Yeah," she says. "The blood reminds me that he's dead."

And the world is a better place, but I don't say that to Mia. Ri was a killer. I saw that in his eyes tonight. He would have killed her. He would have killed again. I help her undress and then do the same. I then walk to the trash can, hit the lever on the floor and trash everything. "I'll get it out of the house after we shower," I say, grabbing her hand and leading her to the shower.

I grab the soap and waste no time making sure I get all remnants of the night off both of us. She needs it all washed away and she needs to rest. "You okay?" I ask when we're just standing there under the spray a few minutes later.

"Because you're here and I'm feeling that twenty-five-year-old whiskey. It's helping. Thank you. I can't believe I saw a man die tonight. I can't believe he was going to kill me and he was. It's—surreal in so many ways."

I stroke a strand of hair from her face. "I know, baby, but it's over and you're safe."

"My father didn't help."

"About that. What happened to not telling him about the bonus Ri gave you to help him?"

"I got angry and I probably misunderstood him, but I didn't think the man I love, who also risked his life to save me tonight, needed to be blamed."

"Come on," I say, turning off the water and grabbing a towel from over the side to wrap it around her. Once she's wrapped up well and I dry my hair and pull a towel around my waist, I lead her to the bedroom.

"Our chair," she whispers.

Our chair. I didn't sit in that damn thing the entire time she was gone. I go there willingly now, and pull her down into it with me, angling us to face each other and pulling the blanket over us. Her fingers splay on my jaw. "I'm glad Blake killed him instead of you. You would have had to live with taking a life, and we both would have known I caused it."

I roll her to her back and settle my leg between hers. "Baby, you did nothing wrong tonight. Nothing."

"Maybe I should have stayed in the office. Maybe I shouldn't have even gone back there at all. I pushed to protect you but you almost got killed tonight."

"You did protect me. You saved me, with Ri and by coming back. I'm the one who wasn't good without you. I needed you, Mia. You belong here with me, and nothing was ever going to be right again until you came back." I lean in and brush my lips over hers and it's all I can do to hold back, to remember how delicate she is tonight. I need to taste her, to feel her, to be inside her.

The instant I pull back, she lifts her head and presses her lips to mine and that's all it takes. My mouth closes down on hers, and I kiss her deeply, intensely, drinking her in, owning her because that's what I need right now. I need to feel her, to know she's here. "You're mine," I whisper, caressing a hand down her back and cupping her backside, pulling her closer. "No one will ever take you again."

"Never again," she promises, her hand on my face, and I drag her leg to my hip, the thick ridge of my erection pressing between her thighs.

"I need to be inside you, but if you—"

"Now would be good," she whispers. "*Now*, please, Grayson."

I press inside her and thrust deep, angling her to take all of me. She gasps out, "You're much, *much* better than whiskey."

I tangle my fingers in her hair and drag her gaze to mine. "Just seeing him hold that gun to your head almost killed me. I'll have nightmares about that for years to come." My mouth closes down on hers and I can't kiss her deep enough, I can't be inside her deep enough. I can't touch her enough or feel her close enough. And yet I go slow, I cradle her hips to my hips. I kiss her neck. I touch her breast and lick her nipple, suckling her until she arches into me. Until she pants out my name.

And those sounds she makes, those soft, sexy sounds drive me crazy and I press my lips to her ear. "I thought I'd never hear you make those sounds again. I thought I'd never hold you like this again. And not just tonight, Mia. I thought I lost you."

"Not for even a moment." She pulls back to look at me. "I was always here in my heart. Always."

My mouth crashes down on hers, and this time, I lose everything but the taste of her, the feel of her, the hunger I cannot sate for this woman, and God knows I tried while she was gone. I tried and failed, and I didn't even want to succeed. I have never been as lost in any other human being, including Mia, as I am lost in her now. The world fades and there is just the two of us and when she shudders in my arms, this time with pleasure, not shock or fear, I follow.

It's long minutes later, that we lay on that chair, clinging to each other, when I tilt her head back and say, "Yes, I would have killed him and I wouldn't have regretted it one day of my life or yours."

LISA RENEE JONES

CHAPTER FORTY-FOUR

Mia

I wake in our chair with Grayson curled around me, his body sheltering me the way I know he tried to do last night, the way he was trying to shelter me even when he fired me from that case, even if he went about it the wrong way. I roll around to face him and find him awake. "How are you?" he asks.

"I'm here. I'm perfect."

One of our phones buzzes somewhere in the distance. "Yours or mine?"

"Probably both. They've been going off for an hour."

"Don't we need to get them?"

"Yes, but I just couldn't make myself get up with you laying here with me." He kisses my temple. "I'll go find our phones." He throws off the blanket and walks across the room and any worry I have is momentarily lost to the sight of his perfect, naked backside.

He disappears into the bathroom and I sit up, pulling the blanket around me. "I don't remember where my purse or briefcase are," I call out.

Grayson exits the bathroom in a pair of pajama bottoms with my robe in his hands. "I don't either actually." He crosses to sit next to me and I eagerly accept the robe as he glances at his phone. "Blake, Eric, Davis, Courtney, and your father have taken turns calling."

"Courtney. Oh God. I didn't even think about calling her."

"I'm texting Courtney and your father in a group text," Grayson says, "Because I need to call Blake first." He looks at me and reads the message he's just typed: *Mac and Courtney, we were asleep. We're fine. Mia lost her phone. We have a few calls to make and then we'll call you both in a few.*

"Perfect," I say. "Hurry and call Blake. I need to pee and I don't want to go until I know what's going on."

"Go, baby. I'll be right here."

"Yeah. I better go." I stand up and race across the room and leave the door open as I hear, "Blake. What's happening?"

Of course, I can hear nothing else and by the time I exit the bathroom, Grayson is meeting me at the door, no longer on the phone. "Blake is having one of his men bring your phone and purse up to us. He had to get it cleared with the police to give it back to you."

"And?"

"And the police will want to interview us again this afternoon. Blake took the liberty of calling our attorney and offering to host the interview at his office. It's a non-event for us, outside of them going after anyone that was helping to set me up." He snags my hand. "Coffee. I need coffee." He starts walking, pulling me along, and I find myself smiling. I love coffee and Grayson, but in our kitchen, together, it's even better.

A few minutes later, we both have steaming cups in our hands and I'm using his phone to assure first Courtney, since she knows nothing at this point, and then my father that all is well when the doorbell rings. Grayson heads for the door and returns with my purse. He's barely handed it to me when my phone starts ringing. "I need to go, dad. I have to return some calls. We'll come see you soon. I love you, too."

I trade Grayson his phone for my purse and quickly pull out my phone "Kevin," I say, "my boss at Ri's firm. He's a good guy. He knew Ri was a problem and he wanted to protect me. I have to call him back, but my client called too, and she must be freaking out. She has to come first but I need some idea of what's on the news and what she's heard."

Grayson grabs the remote and turns on the small TV under the kitchen counter which offers us nothing. "The internet," he says, searching his phone and a few minutes later we both finish reading up on the press which amounts to questions about the future of Ri's firm.

I dial my client. "Mia, what the hell is going on?" she answers. "Are you okay? God, am I okay?"

"I'm fine. You'll be fine. I'm not going back to the firm. I'm—" I look at Grayson, who arches a brow. "I'm going to be with Grayson Bennett's firm. He's my—" I turn away. "We're together. I'm sure you saw that on the news. I want to take you with me but I need to be sure legally I can do that. No matter what I'll take care of you."

"I'm in limbo. Please say that isn't so."

"I'll handle this for you one way or the other. I promise. I'll be in touch by tomorrow." I hang up and Grayson steps in front of me. "I assume I'd come back to the firm. That's okay, right?"

"I wouldn't have it any other way, but let's do this a little differently this time. You don't work for anyone but the firm. Take the cases you want but I'd really like you to work on the bigger picture with me that reaches beyond the firm. Then we can travel together." His hands come down on my arms. "If you want to. I know you want to forge your own career, but you have a brilliant mind and insight I value. You always make me think wider. I'd be lucky to have you work with me as the fourth in my team; you, me, Eric, and Davis."

"I'd like that. I would. I do love criminal law though and I have to take this case all the way. I believe in my client."

"Then you will take it all the way and you'll win. I'll get the case moved. Under the circumstances that won't be an issue. I'll make the calls right after I call a mover to get your things." He folds me against him. "You belong here with me."

"Yes," I say softly, trying not to think about that awkward moment when I didn't know what to call Grayson. "I do."

He strokes my hair from my face. "I'm your future husband," he says. "Don't forget that. I don't plan to."

All those weird feelings fade away. Of course, he's not going to ask me again the morning after we were both covered in a dead man's blood. He's not going to ask me until this is over, because he still doesn't get that I will go to hell and back with him, but I'll have a lifetime to show him that I'm here to stay. I will show him every single day.

CHAPTER FORTY-FIVE

Mia

The rest of the day goes by in a whirlwind of press and chaos. The interviews with the police, however, are uneventful, at least for us. And as Grayson expected, Blake and his team are wonderful. Our team is just as wonderful, including our attorney who I barely know. By the time we leave Blake's office, Grayson has me moved back into the apartment, compliments of a big tip and a moving company. My father stops back by that evening to help us unpack. We're standing in the kitchen, while Grayson takes a few calls in his office, both of us drinking coffee. He tells me about all the new business he has, a woman he might keep seeing, and I pack up some things for him that I don't need now that I'm here.

"Mia," he says, stepping in front of me and taking my hand to shove something in it. "Thank you. I'll never put you in that position again."

I look down and stare at a check for fifty thousand dollars. "The money I owe you."

"You keep it and invest it in your business." I press it back into his hand.

"No. I'm never putting you in that position again. I won't let you make decisions for me."

"And she won't have to," Grayson says, appearing at the bottom of the stairs that lead to his office. He crosses the room to join us, standing beside me, his arm at my waist. "Mia has all the money she could ever need and so do you. Keep the money and we'll talk about how to expand your business."

"No," my father says, holding up his hands. "I never asked you for anything, Grayson. I'm not going to start now."

"But I'm offering and I had planned to offer before Mia and I broke up. We'd talked about it but you're prideful just like your daughter. We'll tread cautiously, but I have money, Mac. Your daughter is the woman I'm going to spend the rest of my life with. We're going to support your business. I want to have Eric look at your books, if you're okay with that. He's got a magical mind. Let him help you with a five-year plan and I'll invest the money."

"No, I—"

"Dad," I say, hugging him. "Let him help." I pull back to look at him. "He really wants to and I didn't ask. He did this himself. Just talk to Eric. Get excited about not struggling anymore."

He looks at Grayson. "I don't know what to say."

"Say you're going to be kinder to my football team this year."

"Damn Patriots," my father grumbles.

Grayson and I laugh. "That is a little kinder than normal," Grayson says, and the two of them head to the balcony with beers in hand to talk about those damn Patriots.

I finish unpacking because I'm home to stay.

The next morning, after much debate, Grayson and I decide that his offices don't need the press we would bring to them but we can't avoid their obsession with us. We agree to a press conference with law enforcement present that is held at Blake's offices. And once again, Grayson shelters me. He takes the heat of the questions for a solid hour before he says enough. Eric takes over from there and we hurry to a car that drives us to the airport for our escape to the Hamptons with not one, but two of Blake's men with us, just to be safe.

By the time we land in the Hamptons and we're in Grayson's Porsche that he's left at the airport, we have the legal approval for us to take over my client's case from Ri's firm. I call my client who is relieved. Next up, is a call to Kevin, my ex-boss, who I've discussed with Grayson in depth. "Mia, how the hell are you?"

"I'm good. Really good. How are you?"

"Afraid for my job. It's not good here."

"Come to work for Bennett. Grayson is going to extend you an official offer for twenty percent higher than you're being paid now."

"Sold. When do I start?"

We work out the details, talk about my client, and then plan to meet at the Bennett offices Monday morning. "I'll arrange to have her there," Kevin promises of my client and we disconnect right as we pull up to the house. "Everything is falling into place," I say, feeling a pinch of sadness. "I remember coming here and it being your father's house he just never used. Now, it's yours."

Grayson pulls us into the garage and parks. "And he'd want me to share it with you." He kills the engine and exits, and by the time I'm standing beside my door, he's there kissing me. He glances at his suit and my dress we'd worn for the press conference. "Let's change and take a walk."

"I'd like that."

A few minutes later, we're both in sweats, tees, and we head to the beach where we start walking. We talk. We talk about everything and then we do it again and as we always do, we end up at the lighthouse. Grayson follows me up the stairs, and we reach the railing just in time to watch the sun begin to lower and streak the darkening sky in orange and red.

Grayson grabs a bottle of wine, and I don't ask where it came from. We always kept wine here. We were always here. He fills two glasses and then offers me one. I sip and sigh. "So many times, I missed us here. So many times when we were here, I just wanted to stay and pretend the rest of the world didn't exist."

He sets our glasses down. "Then stay forever. Stay with me, Mia. Be with me. Be the mother of my children and we will have beautiful babies. You're my best friend, you're my other half. You're a part of me that I can't live without. You know I had to do this here. It didn't feel right anywhere else and yet you feel right in every way." He reaches in his pocket and pulls out my ring and then goes down on his knee. "Will you marry me, Mia?"

Tears prickle in my eyes, and I shake my head. "Yes, a hundred times over. Can we just go do it now, so no one can stop us?"

He stands up and slides the ring on my finger. "No one is going to stop us and you're going to have your perfect wedding, whatever you want that to be."

"The part where we say 'I do' is all I want. I don't care about the rest."

"I do already, baby."

"I do, too." And this time, when he presses me against the wall and kisses me, I don't stop him when he undresses me. I help him because this is our place, this is where I want us to get married. This is where I want our vows to be spoken. This is us.

The End...for now

Would you like to see Grayson and Mia's wedding? And is there a baby in their future? I'll be releasing their "after the happily ever after" book soon!

SIGN-UP TO BE NOTIFIED WHEN MIA AND GRAYSON'S WEDDING BOOK IS AVAILABLE:

https://www.subscribepage.com/betrayal

TURN THE PAGE FOR DETAILS AND INFORMATION ABOUT ERIC'S STORY AND MORE UPCOMING DIRTY RICH WORLD BOOKS INCLUDING GABE'S STORY!

Do you love Eric? His story will play out in THE FILTHY DUET! Book one, THE BASTARD, is available for pre-order and will be out on November 14th!

https://filthyduet.weebly.com/

I'm the bastard child, son to the mistress, my father's backup heir to the Mitchell empire. He sent me to Harvard. I left and became a Navy SEAL, but I'm back now, and I finished school on my own dime. I'm now the right hand man to Grayson Bennett, the billionaire who runs the Bennett Empire. I'm now a few months from being a billionaire myself. I don't need my father's company or his love. My "brother" can have it. I will never go back there. I will never be the mistake my father made, the way he was the mistake my mother made.

And then she walks in the door, the princess I'd once wanted more than I'd wanted my father's love. She wants me to come back. She says my father needs to be saved. I don't want to save my father but I do want her. Deeply. Passionately. More than I want anything else.

But she's The Princess and I'm The Bastard. We don't fit. We don't belong together and yet she says he needs me, that she needs me. We're like sugar and spice, we don't mix, but I really crave a taste. Just one. What harm can just one taste do?

THERE ARE A TON OF DIRTY RICH BOOKS FORTHCOMING THIS YEAR, AND INTO 2019! BE SURE YOU'RE UP TO DATE ON ALL THINGS DIRTY RICH BY VISITING:

https://dirtyrich.lisareneejones.com

SERIES READING ORDER

TURN THE PAGE FOR A SEXY EXCERPT FROM DIRTY RICH OBSESSION – AVAILABLE NOW!

EXCERPT FROM DIRTY RICH OBSESSION

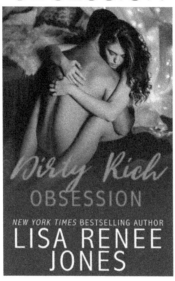

Reid...

I want this woman.

I want her in a bad way, and my tongue licks hungrily into her mouth even as I tighten my grip on her hair. Her hand is warm on my chest, but her elbow is stiff, her entire body is stiff, and I don't accept this from her. I want her submission. I want her to admit she wants like I want, so I deepen the kiss, my hand settling between her shoulder blades, molding her close.

She moans into my mouth, a sexy, aroused sound, but she still fights me. She still shoves weakly at my chest, and her eyes meet mine. "This is just—"

"Hate sex," I supply. "Works for me." My mouth slants over hers again, and this time, she doesn't hold back. She kisses me like she did in that hotel room, her hands sliding under my jacket, over my shirt, and I am hot and hard and ready to be inside her.

I reach up and skim her jacket off her shoulders, my mouth barely leaving hers. I cannot get enough of how she tastes, I damn sure can't get enough of how she feels, and my hands are all over her, caressing her breasts, my finger ripping away a button of her silk blouse.

"You owe me a button and alterations," she hisses, tugging at the buttons of my vest. "And I hate this thing."

I walk her backward and press her against the desk. "And I hate these damn buttons," I say, yanking two more off.

"Reid!"

I snap the front clasp of her bra free.

Her hands go to my arms and I pant out, "I'll buy you another."

"What are we doing, Reid? We work together. You're my—"

"Boss," I supply, cupping her backside and molding her closer. "*Yes.* I am. Start remembering it."

"I remember, and hate that fact, quite well."

"Like you hate me?" I challenge.

"Right now?" she says. "Yes."

I tangle my fingers in her hair again, dragging her mouth to mine, "Exactly why we need to fuck," I say, cupping her breast and pinching her nipple. "So we can both stop thinking about how much we want to be naked together." I kiss her again, swallowing another of her soft, sexy moans while yanking her skirt up her hips, over the lace of her black thigh-highs to her hips.

With that sweet little ass of hers finally bare to my touch, I palm it and squeeze. She yanks hard on my tie, and I have no idea how that makes me hotter and harder, but it does. She does. Every taste of her. Every sound she makes. Everything she does. "Can you just be inside me already?" she demands.

I could, I think. I should want to, but that question, that need in her to just do this and be beyond it and me, grates down my spine in an unexpected way. I don't like it. I turn her and press her to the desk, forcing her to catch herself on the smooth surface. Her ass is perfect, and that too should please me, but it pisses me off. I smack her backside and she yelps, looking over her shoulder.

"Did you really just—"

I yank the red silk of her panties, and the tiny strings rip under my tug. She gasps, and I step into her, smacking her backside again. "Yes," I say, my hand sliding around her, fingers cupping her sex, my lips by her ear. "I did, and," I stroke through the slick wet heat of her sex, "you liked it."

"I didn't—"

I turn her, and kiss her, my tongue doing a quick, deep slide before I demand, "What happened to trust? I can't trust you if you lie to me."

"I don't lie," she says, yanking at my tie again. "Maybe you just think I lie because that's all you know."

"And yet, I never deny anything that feels good the way you just did." I lift her and set her on the desk, spreading her legs and settling on my knees in front of her.

She tries to squeeze her legs together but it's too late. My hands catch her knees, opening her wide. Her eyes meet mine. "You want to pay me back, don't you? That's what this is?"

"You mean lick you until you almost come and then cuff you to the chair and leave you? I could. You wouldn't even stop me." I drag one of her legs over my shoulder, her hips shifting forward, and I lick her clit. "But I'm not going to pay you back," I say, the taste of her on my lips rocketing through my senses. "I want you to come on my tongue again."

"I don't believe you," she whispers, swallowing hard. "I want—"

"Finally, you say it. You want. *I want.*" I lick her again, and she tilts her head back, moaning softly, and that easily she's giving me that submission I want from her. Pushing her to give me more, I suckle her, stroking two fingers along the seam of her sex and then sliding them inside her. She arches her hips, lifting into my mouth, into the pump of my fingers and I love this about her. She's not shy about wanting. She might resist, but once she commits, she's all the way.

"Oh God," she cries out, and then her body is tensing, only seconds before she spasms around my fingers, her legs quaking, and I do own her in this moment. Fuck. I want to own this woman more and that pisses me off. This is a fuck. This is one fuck. I don't ease her into completion. I strip away my fingers and mouth and while she gasps, I shrug out of my jacket, remove my wallet, yank out a condom, and stand up.

Her eyes meet mine with a punch between us that I tell myself is just how badly we both need me to be inside her. That it could be anything else is why I grip her hair, and not gently, reminding her of who is in control. "Now I taste like you again," I say, "but I never forgot how you taste." I close my mouth over hers, a wicked hot kiss, that equals an explosion of lust between us.

I'm kissing her. She's kissing me. My hands are all over her, but hers are on me, too. Stroking my cock through my pants, her fingers driving me crazy. At some point, I rip open the condom and she isn't shy. She's the one that unzips me. She's the one who pulls my erection free, her soft hands stroking along my ridiculously hard length. It's her who puts on the condom and me that cups her backside, pulls her to the edge of the desk and then, when I should just drive into her, fuck her finally, here and now, I tease us both. I stroke my cock along her sex until she hisses, "Enough already. Or not enough. Reid, damn it, I—"

My mouth comes down on hers, my tongue wanting to taste my name on her lips while I press my cock inside her and drive deep, burying myself to the hilt. Our lips part and our foreheads press together, and suddenly we're breathing together, not moving. Why the hell am I not moving? And yet, I'm not. I'm savoring rather than devouring, and that's not what this is. This is sex, hard, ready now sex, and I pull back and thrust into her. She moans, and I drive again, pressing her backward, forcing her to hold onto the desk behind her, not me. But I don't let that become an escape. I'm right here, I'm kissing her. I'm licking her nipple. I'm pumping into her, and yet, it's not enough. I slide my hand between her shoulder blades and lift her off of the desk, holding all of her weight. Somehow we're just there, melded close, and breathing together again, and then kissing again, our bodies more grinding than pumping us into that sweet spot of release.

Carrie gasps and stiffens again, and the minute she begins to orgasm I'm right there with her, my body clenching with the force of my release. I hold her tighter and at some point, I set her back on the desk, gripping it on one side while my other palm remains between her shoulder blades. My face is buried in her neck, and I come back to reality to the feel of her fingers flexing on my shoulders. I want to kiss her again and that is not normal for me. I should pull out. I should end this as fast and hard as we just fucked, and move on, but I don't. What the hell is this woman doing to me? I linger there with her, her body soft and yielding next to mine. I inhale the floral scent of her, and I know, I *know* that I am not done with this woman.

FIND OUT MORE ABOUT DIRTY RICH OBSESSION HERE:

https://dirtyrich.weebly.com/dirty-rich-obsession.html

ALSO BY LISA RENEE JONES

THE INSIDE OUT SERIES
If I Were You
Being Me
Revealing Us
His Secrets*
Rebecca's Lost Journals
The Master Undone*
My Hunger*
No In Between
My Control*
I Belong to You
All of Me*

THE SECRET LIFE OF AMY BENSEN
Escaping Reality
Infinite Possibilities
Forsaken
Unbroken*

CARELESS WHISPERS
Denial
Demand
Surrender

WHITE LIES
Provocative
Shameless

TALL, DARK & DEADLY
Hot Secrets
Dangerous Secrets
Beneath the Secrets

WALKER SECURITY
Deep Under
Pulled Under
Falling Under

LILAH LOVE
Murder Notes
Murder Girl

DIRTY RICH
Dirty Rich One Night Stand
Dirty Rich Cinderella Story
Dirty Rich Obsession
Dirty Rich Betrayal
Dirty Rich Cinderella Story: Ever After (Oct. 2018)
Dirty Rich One Night Stand: Two Years Later (Dec. 2018)
Dirty Rich Obsession: All Mine (Jan. 2019)

THE FILTHY DUET
The Bastard
The Princess

*EBOOK ONLY

ABOUT THE AUTHOR

New York Times and USA Today bestselling author Lisa Renee Jones is the author of the highly acclaimed INSIDE OUT series.

In addition to the success of Lisa's INSIDE OUT series, she has published many successful titles. The TALL, DARK AND DEADLY series and THE SECRET LIFE OF AMY BENSEN series, both spent several months on a combination of the New York Times and USA Today bestselling lists. Lisa is also the author of the bestselling LILAH LOVE and WHITE LIES series.

Prior to publishing Lisa owned multi-state staffing agency that was recognized many times by The Austin Business Journal and also praised by the Dallas Women's Magazine. In 1998 Lisa was listed as the #7 growing women owned business in Entrepreneur Magazine.

Lisa loves to hear from her readers. You can reach her at www.lisareneejones.com and she is active on Twitter and Facebook daily.

CPSIA information can be obtained
at www.ICGtesting.com
Printed in the USA
LVHW09s1811171018
593930LV00001B/87/P

9 781723 921117